BIKINI JONES VS. THE BRAINNAPPERS FROM OUTER SPACE

PATRICK THOMAS

PADWOLF
PUBLISHING

PADWOLF PUBLISHING INC.
WWW.PADWOLF.COM
www.facebook.com/Padwolf

www.patthomas.net

BIKINI JONES VS. THE BRAINAPPERS FROM OUTER SPACE

ISBN 978-1-890096-92-2 First

Printing. Printed in the USA.

Betty Lou grimaced as we both heard the scuttling of hundreds of tiny little legs. "I wish you hadn't said that."

Between us and the end of the chamber, there were dozens of venomous creepy crawlies headed our way, each bigger than my hand.

"Leiurus quinquestriatus!" Betty Lou whispered.

"Deathstalker scorpions!"

"Duh, I just sent that," Betty Lou nagged. "Don't you have some scorpion repellent?"

"Don't you?" I said and tore off my bikini top.

Most people would wonder why I was getting naked at a time like this. I wasn't. Not exactly and Betty Lou knew that.

While most of the time I don't have pockets, what I do have is a bikini. Mrs. Doomhilda's curse made sure that a new bikini appeared on me in a matter of moments once I took one fully off. I found long ago that with a lot of concentration and focus, I could control what the new bikini looked like. In this case, what appeared on me was mirrored metal with a clasp in the front and the back.

I rolled so my back was to Betty Lou and she undid the rear clasps as I opened the front and we each took a cup.

Betty Lou ran her fingers over the material. "Are you sure this is not just going to be burned through by the lasers?"

I shook my head as another mirror surfaced bikini top replaced the first on my chest. "Nope. Only one way to find out."

I lifted my hand in front of the flesh searing beam.

BOOKS BY PATRICK THOMAS

THE MURPHY'S LORE™ SERIES
TALES FROM BULFINCHE'S PUB
FOOLS' DAY
THROUGH THE DRINKING GLASS
SHADOW OF THE WOLF
REDEMPTION ROAD
BARTENDER OF THE GODS

MURPHY'S LORE AFTER HOURS™
NIGHTCAPS
EMPTY GRAVES
THE MUG LIFE

MURPHY'S LORE STARTENDERS™
STARTENDERS
CONSTELLATION PRIZE

MURPHY'S LORE AFTER HOURS™ UNIVERSE
TERRORBELLE:
FAIRY WITH A GUN
FAIRY RIDES THE LIGHTNING
TERRORBELLE THE UNCONQUERED
AGENT KARVER:
RITES OF PASSAGE *(with John French)*
DEAD TO RITES
HELL'S DETECTIVE:
LORE & DYSORDER
BULLETS & BRIMSTONE
(with John French)
THE CASE OF THE MOON MANIAC
(graphic novel with Blair Webb)
HEXCRAFT:
BY DARKNESS CURSED
BY INVOCATION ONLY

SOUL FOR HIRE:
GREATEST HITS

XILES:
EXILE & ENTRANCE

BIKINI JONES
BIKINI JONES VS. THE
BRAINNAPPERS FROM OUT SPACE
BIKINI JONES VS THE
SEA MONSTERS
BIKINI JONES VS THE EMPEROR OF
PLANET Z

DEAR CTHULHU™ SERIES
HAVE A DARK DAY
GOOD ADVICE FOR BAD PEOPLE
CTHULHU KNOWS BEST
WHAT WOULD CTHULHU DO?
CTHULHU HAPPENS
CTHULHU EXPLAINS IT ALL

MYSTIC INVESTIGATORS™ SERIES
MYSTIC INVESTIGATORS
MEAN STREETS
ONCE MORE IN CRIME omnibus
by Patrick Thomas & Diane Raetz
SHADOWS & BRIMSTONES omnibus
by Patrick Thomas & John L. French

GRIFEIN, BATSQUATCH, & DINGBAT:
CRYPTID FIGHT CLUB

AGENTS OF THE ABYSS:
FRANKENSTEIN: MONSTERS OF
THE ABYSS *(with John French)*

PLAYWORLDS:
AS THE GEARS TURN:
Tales of Steamworld

YA:
THE WILDSIDHE CHRONICLES
OMNIBUS *(contributing author)*

ANTHOLOGIES AS CO-EDITOR
NEW BLOOD *(with Diane Raetz)*
CAMELOT 13 *(with John French)*

THE JACK GARDNER MYSTERIES
THE ASSASSAINS' BALL *(with John
French)*

WRITING AS PATRICK T. FIBBS
UNDEAD KID DIARIES™:
OVER MY DEAD BODY
BABE B. BEAR MYSTERIES™:
BAD HAIR DAY
JOY REAPER CHECKS OUT
5 SILLY MONSTERS JUMPING
ON POOR ZED:
an Ughaboos™ picture book
SOGGY GOES TOT THE BEACH
an Ughaboos™ early reader

For Daniel Horne-
for providing the inspiration for Bikini
not to mention the cover

1

My life would be so much simpler if I could just ignore other people's problems. Or other people in general.

Case in point–this morning I decided to go for a walk to get a cup of coffee. It seems a simple enough task to accomplish, but somehow I just couldn't manage it without running into trouble. It would be nice to get a cup of java, then go to work and have the entire trip be boring.

Sadly, it never happens. I got stared at for the whole walk. Since it happens all the time, you'd think I'd be used to it, but you'd be wrong. One of the biggest drawbacks of being cursed to always wear a bikini.

At the coffee shop, five guys and two women offered to buy my java. Only two met my eyes, and neither of them was a woman. Then the barista made my coffee extra slow while staring at me in a mirrored canister. Finally, I made it out of the shop and decided to take the long way to work which is where I came across the little girl holding onto her dog with both hands as two men and a woman in pinstripe suits and carrying dated machine guns tried to separate her from her canine companion.

What did the Tommy Gunners want with a dog?

It was New York City, so everyone else in the street was acting normal and ignoring the whole situation. Did I do that? Did I even try? No, I didn't.

Using stealth techniques I learned in my time studying in a monastery with the Clown Ninja Monks of Newark, I got within throwing distance of the old-school gangsters without them noticing me. Well, not until I threw my cup of coffee in the face of Spats Magool, the gangster who was pointing her machine gun at the little girl's head.

I didn't waste time trying to take the gun away from her. Instead, I reached out and took the drum cylinder from the Tommy gun and threw it down a sewer grate, then regretted it. I wasn't sure what caliber weapons the mole women or the samurai alligators were using these days, but they hardly needed more ammo.

I used the *I got your nose nerve pinch* on the mobster and she hit the ground snoring. The other two gangsters recognized me, then shoved the little girl into traffic and ran off toward the corner, carrying the small dog.

I dove after the girl, grabbing hold of her midway through a somersault. Once back on my feet, I looked up just in time to see an ancient orange Pinto coming at us. Still holding her, I leaped up to land on the hood, then ran up the windshield onto the roof of the car. Another jump landed us on a parked car where we dropped to the sidewalk.

"Are you okay?"

The girl sniffed through her tears and nodded. "Yeah, but they got Mr. Cuddles."

"I'll get Mr. Cuddles back for you. Do you have any clue why the Tommy Gunners would want your dog? Did you find a dog collar with a jewel on it or something?"

The girl shook her head. "No, I have no idea."

A Wall Street looking type in an expensive suit and carrying a pricey briefcase had stopped in his Gucci tracks to stare at me. His gaze was nowhere near my face. I clapped my hands in front of his eyes, stopping him from making me his personal peep show.

"What's your name?" I demanded.

"Danny McTain. Why? You want my number?"

"In your dreams. I want you to dial 911 and let them

know what's going on here, then keep an eye on this little girl until I get back."

"Listen, lady, I don't know what your problem is, but I ain't babysitting your kid for you, no matter how hot you look in that bikini. You couldn't afford me. Besides, if you ain't giving me your digits, I gotta get to work," McTain said.

Using pickpocket skills honed on the streets of Newark, Tokyo, and Milwaukee, I reached inside his suit pocket and pulled out his wallet and work ID while he whined.

"Danny McTain, if you don't make the call and are not still here when I come back to check on the girl, I'll let your wife and mistress know you're cheating on them."

"How do you…"

I sprinted down the street, not waiting for him to finish his question. It was hardly my job to explain to him I could tell he was packing two cell phones and had a mark where a wedding ring had just been taken off.

I did my best to ignore the stares of the men and the scowls of the women that my sprinting in a bikini was causing. I was fortunate it was a sports bikini with extra support.

Instead of heading for the corner they had just turned on, I took a shortcut into an alley. I've never been a fan of cigarette smoking but I wasn't about to complain about the ashcan on top of the trash bin at the end of the alley. I scooped the metal dish up, hit the street, and turned toward the corner the gangsters should still be heading toward. I waited until the two remaining Tommy Gunners got close. Luckily, they were looking for me behind them, not in front. I flung the ashes and cigarette butts toward their faces, which made them flinch and shut their eyes long enough for me to hit the tips of the barrels with my hands.

I stood and waited until they recovered. Joey Capone, who was the smaller of the two, held the dog. Joey claimed to be the reincarnation of Al Capone's grandson, which always seemed a somewhat pointless claim. The larger guy who made linebackers look tiny had the appropriate moniker of Big Lug. Lug was strong enough to rip apart the New York City phone book, if you could find one these days. They pointed their Tommy guns at me. When I didn't flinch or move, they got nervous. When I smiled, they rolled their eyes.

"Oh, come on! You didn't do it again?" Joey Capone said.

"Pull the trigger and find out." Last time we tangled I managed to get some quick hardening epoxy into the tubes of both their guns so when they fired the barrels exploded and shrapnel came back at them. I made sure they felt me move the guns and since neither could see at the time, they wouldn't know I'd had nothing in my hands. I'm a damn good poker player–I'd been banned at casinos in Vegas, Monte Carlo, and the Vega System–but I was even better at bluffs like this.

"Come on, Bikini, these organ grinders are antiques. They cost a fortune to replace," Joey Capone whined.

"You could just go straight. Or update your weaponry."

"The straight life ain't for us."

"But boss, I like dames," Big Lug said.

"Not that kind of straight, you palooka. The straight and narrow," Joey Capone said.

Big Lug nodded. "That's good, boss, because I like you fine but not in that way."

Joey Capone rolled his eyes.

"So how about you put down your guns and come along quietly this time?" I said.

"The Tommy Gunners don't go down without a fight," Joey Capone shouted.

"Spats did." The guy I got with the nose pinch.

"But, Boss, when we fight Bikini, we always end up losing. It's embarrassing getting beat up by a broad. The other guys in prison always make fun of me." Big Lug sniffled and wiped the corner of his eyes. "It hurts my feelings when they do that."

Lug was so simple and desperate for approval that I couldn't help but feel bad for him. "I'm sorry to hear that that happens to you, Lug."

"That's awful nice of you to say, Ms. Bikini, but it ain't your fault. You is just a better fighter than I is. I don't understand why I can never beat you cause I'm bigger and stronger."

"I'm faster and practice more." I almost said smarter, but it would have only hurt Big Lug's feelings. I knew the reason he stays with the Tommy Gunners is that Joey and Spats are his only friends. And in all fairness, they're old-school villains. They've never killed anyone during one of their crimes. In fact, they use rubber bullets that hurt like hell but don't break the skin. They knew I would save the girl when they pushed her out in traffic. Give me a thousand Tommy Gunners over one of those morons who love to leave a trail of bodies in their wake.

"So why are you guys resorting to dognapping? You don't have to steal a pet. Just go to the pound and you can adopt one."

Big Lug got a huge grin on his face. "Boss, that sounds like fun. Can we adopt a dog that I can take home and love and call Mookie?"

"You're yammering crazy. Who's gonna walk it and give it baths?" Joey Capone said.

"I could do that. I like walks. Baths I'm not too crazy about, but I'll figure something out."

"Who's going to take care of the dog when we're in stir? Do you ever think about that, you big palooka?" Joey Capone reached up and slapped the large man upside his skull.

Big Lug rubbed his head and frowned. "No. Maybe we can go straight and then we wouldn't have to go to prison."

"Ain't you listening, ya bum? I already said the straight life ain't for us!"

"How do you know, Boss? We ain't never tried. Please? We always do the stuff you and Spats want to do like rob and steal, but we never do what I want. I really want a dog and I've been good for a real long time."

Joey Capone sighed. "I know you have, Lug, but as the reincarnated grandson of Al Capone, I got a legacy to uphold. What would Gramps say if I went straight?"

"I know what Capone would say if he was alive today," I said.

Joey Capone's jaw dropped, and his eyebrow's shot up. "You do?"

I nodded. "He'd say, *Let me out of this coffin. I ain't dead!*"

Big Lug snickered but stopped short after a glare from Joey.

"You are aware that Al Capone didn't limit himself to criminal enterprises, right?"

Now Joey looked confused. "What'd you mean?"

"He had a bunch of legitimate businesses too. If you could run a successful business, I'd have to guess that your grandfather…" Note I didn't say Al Capone. "… would probably be very proud of you."

"What can we do? All we knows is crime."

"Not true. You're an expert on the prohibition era." Joey Capone used to be Professor Joseph Capponelli, a renowned specialist in American history from the turn-of-the-last-century to the end of World War II but that was before he hit his head during a tour of Al Capone's vault and woke up thinking he was the reincarnated grandson of a gangster. "Theme restaurants are all the rage again. You could open a speakeasy-themed restaurant. Make it reservation only. When people make a reservation, they get a password and have to use it at the door to get in. The waiters and waitresses could play the parts of gangsters and molls. There are enough unemployed actors and actresses in New York who wouldn't mind combining earning a living with a little acting," I said.

"That sounds like fun! We wouldn't have to go to the big house no more and I could get a dog," Big Lug said.

Joey shrugged. "It's a nice dream, but where would we get the cabbage?"

"We both know you have the largest collection of 1920s and 30s memorabilia in the world. You can take a couple of your more expensive items and auction them off and use the money for the restaurant. Then you could set up displays so you can show the rest your collection off to the public. Maybe put in a museum next to the restaurant and charge people to look at it. Do it right and maybe you can have schools come on field trips."

"It's going to be kind of hard to do that from the slammer," Joey Capone said. "We won't go down without a fight, but without any heaters, we know how this is going to end–with you sending us to the big house."

"Well, dognapping doesn't normally carry a lot of jail time. Maybe you can explain what the point of all this is," I said.

"We need his help on a job."

"Whose help? The dog?" The gangsters nodded. "What kind of job would you need a dog for? Planning on robbing the receipts at the Westminster Dog Show?"

"Whoa! That would've been a good idea," Big Lug said. "Are you sure you wouldn't want to join our gang, Bikini?"

"I'm sure. Besides, I could never wear the uniform." I can't wear anything. The curse makes sure that any clothes I put on that cover my bikini disappear within seconds. It sucks. "So what was the plan?"

Joey Capone looked at his well-shined shoes. "We was going to knock over Fort Knox."

"Again?" I said.

Joey Capone smiled and shrugged his shoulders. "Hey, third times the charm."

"Why would you need this dog?"

"Because he's a genius," Joey Capone said.

"This dog?" I looked closely at the dog for the first time. Beneath the fur, there was a familiar circular incision and stitch pattern over the top of his head. "Dr. Dendrite?"

"Crap," the dog said and nipped at Joey's hands, but the mobster wouldn't let go so the dog lifted his leg and peed on the Tommy Gunner's face. Joey threw the dog on the ground, and doggy Dendrite ran. I dumped the garbage out of a can and threw it over the dog before he'd gotten twenty feet.

"You're telling me that Dr. Dendrite transplanted his brain into a normal dog?" The mad scientist had put his brain in people, robots, a yeti, and even a cloned T-Rex. Choosing a small canine didn't make any sense.

Big Lug nodded. "Yup."

"Is he hoping to take over the world as a dog?"

"He ain't. The doc went straight, but he owes us ever since we got him that sasquatch corpse to put his brain in," Joey Capone said. Dendrite was a mad scientist, but old school, same as the Tommy Gunners. He'd never killed to get a body. He could revitalize dead ones.

"But then you turned me in for the reward!" rang out the voice of the dog from beneath the garbage can.

A TV show had offered a million-dollar reward for anyone who could prove the existence of Bigfoot. Joey Capone got it, then spent it all on gangster memorabilia.

"Hey, we got you the corpse as a favor. We had to get paid too."

I knocked on the top of the garbage can, and Dr. Dendrite howled. "Be quiet. I'm going to lift the garbage can. If you try to run away, you will regret it, understand?"

"I have a 247 IQ. Of course, I do."

I motioned for Big Lug to lift the can. He put his Tommy gun down on the ground and did as requested. As soon as the rim rose high enough, the little dog made a run for it, but I caught him by the scruff of his neck and lifted him up.

The little stinker tried to bite me, so I wrapped my hand around his small jaws and squeezed it tight. The dog whimpered and tried to pull away, but it didn't work. "Bad move, Dr. D. You would have broken the skin, which means I would have had to call the pound. There's the death penalty in this state for a dog that bites people."

"You wouldn't," he mumbled through clenched jaws.

"Bite me and find out." I grinned and let go of his mouth. "Or maybe we can take you in and have you fixed. It wouldn't be too hard to find a muzzle."

"Fine. I have no plan. I truly have gone straight."

"Why now? What's changed?"

The dog stopped looking me in the face, and his gaze shifted down toward his paws. "It's personal."

"I'm just supposed to accept what you tell me and let you live with that little girl? What is she? A mutant? Alien Princess? The seventh daughter of a seventh daughter?"

The mutt shook his head. "No, she's just a normal

average girl. Now let me go so I can get back to her."

"Not until you convince me she isn't a cog in one of your plans for world domination. Besides, aren't you still wanted somewhere?"

"I am not. The World Court gave me immunity and time served after I switched back the brains of the president and all the prime ministers and premieres that the lizard people had placed the mutant iguana brains into. Although to be honest, I think they were all doing a better job with the iguana brains than the human ones. But in recognition of my service, all charges and warrants against me were dropped, which means I'm starting with a clean slate. As long as I don't do anything criminal, I'm just a regular person."

"Regular people don't have four legs, a tail, and pee on people's faces."

"Actually, there is this place downtown..." Joey Capone said.

I held my hand up. "Hush. I don't want to hear about it."

"Mary Sue..."

That ticked me off. "Dendrite, you don't get to call me by my real name. You lost that privilege the first time you tried to kidnap my mom." Dr. Dendrite and my mom had worked together years ago. Worse, they even dated before she met my dad. Oddly enough, he was a friend of the family who was always around, including at my sister and my birthday parties. He'd been practically an uncle.

"Let me go back to her. *Please.*"

I've known Dr. Dendrite for a long time. Since he went bad, I've never heard him utter the word please, not even when he was dangling over the rim of an active volcano and wanted me to pull him up. I took a deep breath. "You swear you don't mean the girl or anyone associated with her any harm? And it's nothing creepy?"

"I swear. And I can prove I've changed. I've amassed a fortune over the years, much of it obtained legally through patents or surgical equipment. I'll put up half of what the Tommy Gunners need for their theme restaurant."

Dr. Dendrite rattled off a large number.

Joey Capone's eyebrows raised at the large number. "How do you know we'll need that much?" The dog rolled his eyes. "Please. Mega-genius here."

Joey Casanova narrowed his eyes. "What you want for that scratch?"

"Twenty percent ownership in the restaurant and the loan paid back in five years with interest two percent above prime." Joey started to open his mouth. "You are all known criminals and felons. No one else is going to give you a loan at less than ten percent above prime."

"True. The few items I'd be willing to part with would cover half of what's left. But where would we get the rest of the dough?" Joey Capone asked.

"Maybe Bikini could loan it to us," Big Lug suggested.

I felt my eyebrows move toward my hairline. "Are you serious?"

Lug smiled. "Well, Bikini it was your idea and you're always telling us how we should go straight. If you give us the money..."

"Loan."

"... Loan us the money, we'll give you ten percent ownership and pay you back at three percent above prime in five years," Big Lug said.

Dendrite barked, then said, "Three percent?! Wait a second..."

"No way are we going into business with our sworn enemy," Joey shouted.

"Boss, think about it. If Bikini owns a piece of it, she'd

probably be willing to help us out. She's really smart."

The dog snorted and the self-proclaimed mega-genius ignored the glare I sent his way. "I'll give you she's a *slightly* above average genius."

I thought about it. I had a *lot* of extra money since I found that sunken pirate treasure on the moon and brought back those diamonds from Jupiter. And my Bikini Enterprises was turning a decent profit, no small feat since I have a tendency to spend everything that comes in to help others and on research through my Bikini Foundation charity. Big Lug was right, I was always trying to convince the bad guys to go good. It appeared I had no choice but to put my money where my mouth was.

"Fine, I'll loan you the money. But I get twelve percent and approval on the site so we can make sure that there will be enough traffic to support this restaurant. And, I want to see a five-year business plan before I write you a check."

Joey Capone took a deep breath. "I don't know nothing from business plans."

"Don't worry, I do." All of us stared at Big Lug. "I have an MBA. I graduated summa cum laude from Yale on a full scholarship. When I want something, I'm willing to work hard for it. I find sometimes that hard work makes up for me not being as smart as everyone else."

"So Dr. D, how's we going to pay youse back?"

"'How are we going to pay you back' is the proper vernacular," Dendrite said, correcting Joey's grammar.

"That's what I said. So, can you cash a check as a dog?"

"I don't want you to pay it back to me. Pay it into a trust fund for Harper Dennis. That's the kid." The dog and I shared a look, and he nodded. I finally understood why he was a dog. Turns out, he was probably telling the truth.

"I'll take you back to Harper," I said, taking the drum magazines off the old-time machine guns. "You two and Spats call my assistant and stay out of trouble. Pull any crime or job and the deal's off, capiche?"

Big Lug nodded, then jumped up and down clapping.

Joey nodded. "Capiche."

"Thanks, Bikini," Big Lug said.

"You're welcome. And Big Lug is an equal partner to you and Spats or no deal."

The Tommy Gunner nodded.

"Joey, can we go to the pound today to pick out a dog, please?"

The mobster boss sighed. "Sure."

Big Lug picked Joey Capone up off the ground and gave him a hug that would make a bear envious. Joey looked like he couldn't breathe.

"I could have loaned them the entire amount you know," doggie Dendrite said.

"So why didn't you?" I said.

"They fear me, but they don't respect me. They would be far more afraid of disappointing you. It will make them toe the line and succeed."

"That's awful nice of you."

"I suppose. I don't have people who I'm close to, but those three morons might be the closest thing I have to…" Dendrite paused as if unsure what word to use, very unusual for the self-proclaimed mega-genius.

"Friends?" I offered.

Dendrite huffed and turned his furry head away, doing his best to ignore me.

2

"You rescued Mr. Cuddles! Thank you so much!"

Harper was thrilled to get her dog back. Danny McTain was thrilled he could leave and go to work.

The young girl took the dog out of my hands and showered his furry face with kisses. Next, she rubbed behind his ears before setting him down on the cement sidewalk and rubbing his belly. The dog's tail started wagging like a helicopter rotor. Dendrite glanced at me out of the corner of his canine eye and seemed embarrassed.

"I left his leash where they grabbed him. Will you watch Mr. Cuddles for me for a minute so I can get it?"

"Sure."

Harper ran down the block. I crossed my arms over my chest and smirked at the dog with the human brain. Dendrite looked up at me and scowled.

"Don't you judge me. Dogs are wired differently than a human. That's a natural reaction to getting petted."

I was going to ask another question, but Harper came back and I didn't want to blow Dendrite's cover.

The girl hooked the leash onto *Mr. Cuddles'* collar and grinned at me. "Thank you, Bikini Jones."

"You know I am?"

"I don't have to be a detective like you to figure that out. I mean, you are wearing a bikini and it's fifty-five degrees out. Not many people do that. Don't you get cold?"

"Only a little." I've gotten used to it over the years. When it gets too cold, I have wrist and ankle heaters plus a special hat.

"Would you take a selfie with Mr. Cuddles and me?

Then I could blow it up and put it next to the poster of you I have in my room."

"I thought only boys bought that poster." It was something I did a few years ago when I wasn't quite as flush with money as I am now. It paid off my mortgage and funded medical clinics in three different countries.

"I have it up because I admire you. You're a role model and a hero. It's not your fault that a mean witch's curse makes you always have to wear a bikini. You have four doctorates, black belts in seven different martial arts, been a professional racecar driver, detective, fighter jet pilot, and astronaut."

I was up to five doctorates, but the rest of it was pretty much on the money.

"When I grow up, I want to be just like you. Except with more clothes."

I laughed. "I wouldn't mind being able to do that myself."

Harper picked up Mr. Cuddles and put him between us. We leaned in and smiled as she took a selfie. Well, Harper and I did. The undercover Dr. Dendrite was scowling and giving me a dirty look.

"What happened to those men?" Harper said.

"It was a case of mistaken identity. We worked things out, and they gave Mr. Cuddles back once they realized their error."

"Are they going to jail?"

"Since they gave him back and didn't hurt him, I let them off with a warning. And I think I may have talked them out of a life of crime. We'll see if it takes."

"If you think it's best. It was awesome to meet you."

"You too, Harper."

"How do you know my name?"

I recovered quickly. "Detective, remember? You and Mr. Cuddles take care."

"We will. Say goodbye, Mr. Cuddles." Harper used her hand to wave his paw, but doggy Dendrite just rolled his eyes.

I waved back and left.

3

I decided to head into the office where I could at least get a replacement cup of coffee. Before I got half a block, camera lightning filled the air. There was a paparazzo following me.

"Bikini, over here! Marvin from the Weekly Tattle. Is it true you're dating a yeti?"

I sighed. This guy must be new. "No, we're just friends."

"Then you're confirming the existence of yeti?"

I ignored him and kept walking. Marvin kept shooting pictures and video. Some time ago, I got tired of constantly being featured in newspapers and tabloids for the cheesecake factor and comments about what bikini the curse's magic had whipped up for me that day. Instead of whining, I did something about it. Turns out digital and video cameras get messed up by infrared light and low frequencies on the magic spectrum. By mixing the two, I whipped up special earrings and a brooch that fit on the clasp in front of my top and one for the front and back of my bikini bottom.

They all emit specially designed rays which ensures that whenever I get photographed, I show up as a glowing blur, blocking out my face and the parts that sell newspapers. At first, it led to stories about me being a ghost or an alien, but those went away after a while.

I went to Bikini Tower, my very own skyscraper. The top five floors make up my offices. I'd like to say that I managed to save up enough to buy or build it on my own but the truth is I won it in a poker game in Atlantic City, playing against a real estate tycoon, Count Dracula, and the Empress of Saturn. I also got a shuttlecraft and

Dracula's favorite coffin, which came complete with a force field and was amazingly comfortable.

When I got to the front, a cute dumpling of an octogenarian smiled and opened the door.

"Good morning, Sherman. How're the grandkids?"

"Simply wonderful, Ms. Jones. How are you today? An uneventful morning, I hope," Sherman said, straightening his long doorman jacket and hat.

"Don't I wish," I said.

"I don't wish anymore since that episode with the genie," Sherman said.

"Nonsense. You're the only one who didn't use his wishes for selfish reasons and you ended up fixing the whole mess."

"Well, Ms. Jones, you know I like things to run nice and orderly."

I always let Sherman get away with one Ms. Jones a day, but that was his second. "Sherman, how many times have I told you just to call me Bikini? Or even Mary Sue?"

"3,117. That I can recall."

"And when are you going to start doing it?"

Sherman grinned. "Any day now, Ms. Jones."

"You're lucky you're so cute."

"Not to mention the best doorman in all of Manhattan. You couldn't replace me at twice the price."

"I couldn't replace you at any price, Sherman. And I wouldn't say you were the best doorman in Manhattan."

Sherman's smiley face plummeted into a frown. "You wouldn't?" The old man looked like he was about to cry.

"No, I wouldn't. I would say you're the best doorman in the entire world."

Sherman's smile returned along with some rosy cheeks. "That's mighty kind of you to say, Ms. Jones.

Don't nobody get by me while I'm on duty."

"That's true." Sherman had been rebuilt as a cyborg and was stronger than a dragon. The laser beams he could shoot out of his eyes and fingers didn't hurt either.

"Have a wonderful day, Ms. Jones."

"Thank you, Sherman. You give my best to your grands."

"Will do."

Marvin the paparazzi made the mistake of coming into the building after me.

All five foot five of Sherman stepped in front of the six-foot-tall tabloid reporter. "State your business please."

Marvin didn't even look at Sherman. "Back off, buddy. I'm the press and I'm here to talk to Bikini."

Sherman turned to where I was waiting for the elevator. I shook my head.

Sherman stepped closer. "Well, Ms. Jones is not seeing you. Kindly exit the premises."

"This is a business. You can't keep me out."

"If only I were a betting man." The tabloid reporter rushed forward, expecting to plow past the old man but instead ended up bouncing off of Sherman and landing butt-first on the floor.

Before the reporter could say anything, Sherman's metal left wrist telescoped to grab hold of the man's cameras.

"Hey, those are mine. They cost more than you make in a month."

"Probably not." I saw Sherman point his left index finger at the cameras and I saw the tiniest flash of light. It was a focused EMP–electromagnetic pulse–which means Sherman fried the camera's memory cards. The doorman was very protective of me and for that I was appreciative.

"This is not a business that is open to the public, so you are trespassing. If you would like me to give you back your cameras and not call the police, you'd best walk out the door right now under your own power."

"And if I don't?"

"Are you familiar with the term bum's rush? If you're not, Google it. I'll wait," Sherman said.

That's when my elevator dinged and I got on, confident that Sherman had matters well in hand. Bikini Tower wasn't big by New York standards, only forty-two floors–at least above ground. I was the only tenant and believe it or not, I found a use for most of the space. A lot of it was storage or living space, but even more was research and development.

Despite what you may have heard, I'm not always comfortable in my own skin. I know there are a lot of men and women who look down at me because I'm stuck in a bikini all the time and they think I'm showing off. Those people have never been picked apart on a morning talk show for having cellulite. Forget about social media. I have to diet and exercise constantly and I haven't been a teenager for years.

"Morning, Boss," Hany said, dressed in a power business suit. I may have been the CEO of Bikini Enterprises, but Hany ran it and did a fantastic job. We have two purposes. One is developing products and endorsements. The other is running the Bikini Foundation charities around the world.

Hany had been kidnapped by the Flying Dutchman back in 1832. Although kidnapped might not be the best word. She'd only been eight years old at the time and the ghost ship offered her a way off the plantation where she was a slave so she took it. Turns out the sailors on the ghost ship were very good to her and she grew up happy, but slowly. Hany had only aged about 20 years while almost two hundred had passed in the living world. When the captain of the Flying Dutchman asked me to take her back to the mortal realm, Hany was lost in a strange time and a strange place. She asked me for a job. She started in the mailroom and worked her way up to running the place.

"Typical morning. You're going to be contacted by Joey Capone, Big Lug, and Spats of the Tommy Gunners."

"Ransom demand?"

"No. We're going to be investing in a theme restaurant but with conditions. I'll send you a memo later regarding what they are."

Hany nodded and made a note on her clipboard. She loathed tablets. She's proficient in using her phone but felt electronics took away from writing down things on paper which is how she organized. As she planned a large part of my life, I had no complaints.

"Just want to let you know that the Bikini Pitcher prototype should be ready by the end of the month."

"Wow, that soon?" We had a clean water initiative. There are a horrendous number of people in the world who have water that's not safe to drink, so we were developing a pitcher that would filter out sentiments and chemicals of bad water and disinfect for any bacteria and viruses along with several other hazards. The initial plan was for the pitchers but eventually, I wanted it to come out in bucket and barrel sizes. "That's great but we don't have to put my name in front of everything you know. I don't have a Bikinimobile or a Bikinicave."

"Branding is everything. With your name on it, people will trust it and we'll get it into the hands of those whose lives it may save faster. Plus, the initial design was yours and things have progressed even faster since you convinced the Atlantean scientists to consult with us. Soon the Bikini Pitcher will be able to filter seawater as well."

"I'll have to send Scalon a thank you text."

"You may be able to do more than that. The Prince of the Merpeople has invited you to a ball in the Sunken Palace next weekend."

"As a guest or as his date?"

"He knew you would ask that question and said whichever you like but his preference would be as his date," Hany said.

I sighed. "He's a great guy and the top half of him is gorgeous but the tail kind of makes me take a big step back."

"It's not that big of a deal. The important equipment is still there," Hany said.

I raised an eyebrow. "Are you speaking from experience?"

Hany blushed. "I did spend nearly two centuries above the seas and larger lakes of the world. I did date this one merlad, and he was wonderful. Do you know that if a merperson kisses you, you can breathe underwater for an hour?"

Now was my turn to blush. "Actually, I do. Let's move on. What's on the agenda for today?"

"At ten, you meet with the designer for your new swimwear line. At two you meet with the toy company to discuss renewing the licensing for your doll and action figure lines."

"They look pretty close. What's the difference again?"

"Marketing. Some people don't like the idea of boys playing with dolls so by calling them action figures it makes it okay. Ridiculous, I know but the money it brought in last year helped rebuild an entire town in Haiti after the hurricane."

"Then we knock off at six because it's our monthly

girls' night."

"That sounds great."

"Bikini, you've got a call," said Stanley. My personal assistant was good at taking care of busy work and not bothering me unless it was important. "You're probably going to want to take it."

"Why? Is it the president?"

"No, your sister."

I sighed.

"Aren't you two feuding this week?" Hany said.

"I don't know. It happens so often that I lose track, but I think so."

"Then a call during a feud week means Betty Lou probably needs your help."

"Which she hates to ask for, even when we're getting along."

"What joy awaits. And with that, I'll take my leave of you and get back to work," Hany said.

"Thanks." On her way up the corporate ladder here, her last stop before running the place was as my last personal assistant, so she knew my life even better than Stanley. She still insists on doing my morning intake.

"Stanley, I'll take it on the screen in my office."

4

Iwent into my office and hit a button that shaded the glass walls to give me some privacy. As a kid, I loved shows where the heroes would get to talk on a giant screen so I had one had installed in my office. Anyone with a cell phone can call, but it looks cooler on a two-hundred-inch TV.

"Hi, Mary Sue."

"Hi, Betty Lou. I thought you weren't speaking to me?"

"I shouldn't be."

"Why again?"

"You know darn well why. You stole another one of my boyfriends."

"I didn't steal your boyfriend. He was on his phone most of the time, chewed with his mouth open, and helped himself to Dad's five hundred dollar bottle of Scotch that he was saving to open on the day his first grandchild was born. Oh, and he spent the entire dinner at Mom and Dad's staring at my cleavage."

"Can you blame him when you sat right in front of him dressed in next to nothing?"

"You know it's not my fault."

"I don't know. Maybe you shouldn't have been prancing around in a bikini in front of Mr. Doomhilda."

"I wasn't prancing around. I was sunbathing in *our* backyard and he was staring through a knothole in the fence when his wife caught him. Instead of being mad at him. she took his creepy peeping tomness out on me."

It was just my luck that she was one of the most powerful witches in the world. In a jealous rage, Doomhilda cursed me to forever be as I was that day, wearing a bikini. She claimed it was some sort of lesson to teach me to not tempt married men with my feminine wiles. Her words, not mine. And to this day I still have no idea how being stuck forever in a two-piece bathing suit was supposed to teach me that lesson. Or anything for that matter.

"You could've covered up."

"Betty Lou, you know as well as I do that isn't an option for me. Maybe your BF should've shown some manners and been respectful of the woman he was dating by not ogling her sister. And honestly, Sis, you dress like an uptight Victorian librarian. Not every outfit you wear has to come to two inches above your clavicle. You're a good-looking woman. You shouldn't be so reluctant to show it."

"Yeah right. Not all of us look like you do."

"Do you know how hard I have to work to stay fit? I'm against people body-shaming for any reason and that includes people who happen to look good. If that's why you called, we can just end this conversation and go back to not speaking."

"I wish, but I need your help. Something weird is going on at my dig site."

"I think it's amazing that you found an Egyptian pyramid in a small town barely an hour outside of Philadelphia."

"It wasn't so much me as the people who were building a strip mall on former farmland. We were lucky enough to see the picture they posted on Instagram and stop them before they destroyed it."

"You have a doctorate in archaeology and quantum physics, not to mention a degree in molecular biology. I can't imagine something at a dig that you can't handle."

"That's kind of you to say, but we both know my degree in molecular biology is only a Masters. Not all of us can acquire doctorates as fast as you can."

"I've offered you the use of the stasis sphere." It's not so much a time machine as a way to accomplish a lot in a short period. Inside you don't age or have to eat or sleep. For every year that passes inside only a few hours passed outside. Whenever I need to learn something, I go into the sphere and it typically takes me about five or fewer minutes in real time to do it. It's how I've earned so many doctorates and still keep up my adventurer's lifestyle.

"I find the differential in the parallel flow of time disturbing. I'm not convinced there won't be some sort of chronological payback down the line resulting in instant aging. Besides, I've yet to be persuaded that you won't wander off and forget about me being in there."

"When have I ever wandered off without you?"

"Homecoming."

"Being kidnapped by a squad of zombie cheerleaders is not the same as wandering off."

"There is no proof of that."

"It was on the news!"

"You could have dug up those girls."

"Why would I dig up five dead girls and put them in cheerleading uniforms? And how would I animate them?"

"Let's agree to disagree."

"That accounts for most of our relationship."

"True. The problem is women in this town have been disappearing. Just women. I didn't even hear about it from the cops until my assistant Jenny vanished last night. I called the police, and she's the fifth woman to have gone missing in the neighborhood surrounding the dig site."

"You didn't let loose a mummy? Or forget to deactivate a curse before you opened the pyramid?"

"I wouldn't do that." Betty Lou raised her nose indignantly, then looked down, unable to meet my eyes. "At least not again. The mummy was the regular variety, and I deactivated the curse and double-checked it before anyone crossed in. The mummy remains inanimate. I know you're busy but I was hoping you would come help. Jenny is more than an assistant. She's a friend and I don't think the cops are going to be able to find her. If anyone can find a missing person, it's you. I'm just hoping she'll still be alive by then."

"You know all you have to do is ask, Betty Lou. I like Jenny too. I'll be there within the hour."

"But you're in New York…"

"Don't worry about it. I'll see you soon."

5

I hung up and moved to hit the intercom button. Stanley seemed to have materialized in front of me.

"You rang?"

"How'd you do that?"

"I was raised by psychics," Stanley said.

"Really? Why is this the first I'm hearing about it?"

"Because I'm being sarcastic. Since you are feuding, your sister would only call you because she needed help. Your type of help can't be done over the phone. Therefore you're on your way to Philadelphia. Shall I have them warm up the helicopter or send for the Saturnian shuttlecraft? I'll cancel your meetings with the swimwear designer and the toy people."

"No, don't cancel them. You and Hany go and give the designs your once over. You both know me well enough to have an idea of what I like. Get things narrowed down for me to choose from."

Stanley straightened his skinny tie. "Right boss. Thanks for your confidence."

"You're welcome. And I don't think I'm going to take the helicopter or the shuttlecraft. I just got a new toy I want to try out."

6

"Whee!" I've been lucky enough to have flown everything from an interstellar battlecruiser to a lawn chair with a balloon and a battery-powered fan that I made when I was sixteen. I've even ridden a pterodactyl with a saddle.

The foo fighter beat them all. It handled in the air better than any machine I've ever been in. It was literally a ball of light. To me, it seemed like magic and it was made by a hidden sect of the Fey called the Foo. They've used them several times on Earth, most notably during World War II.

Their chief magicologist had his twin children kidnapped by a villain who wanted Foo Fey technology. I managed to get the kids back safe and sound. As a thank you, they gave me my very own foo fighter. The controls worked with a combination of body movements and thought. It seemed to break the laws of physics and could make a ninety-degree turn even moving at several times the speed of sound without any G-forces to the pilot.

It was quite possibly one of the fastest craft in the solar system and likely the most maneuverable. This was my first time taking it through its full paces. On Earth at least. I could've made it a few minutes sooner, but I took a little detour by way of San Francisco and back. All in all, it was less than half an hour from when I hung up with my sister to when I landed at the Pennsylvania pyramid.

The foo fighter didn't have a GPS as such but I could just think about a place and it took me there. Very impressive.

Betty Lou was waiting outside the pyramid with some other people as I slowly dropped out of the sky and landed in front of her.

The one drawback with the foo fighter is that it has no security systems. It was supposed to be keyed to my DNA, but anyone could just stick their head inside and look around. I'm not convinced someone couldn't figure out a way to hijack it. It had a homing function so once I stepped out, I activated it and used my phone watch to signal the hanger team that it was on the way back. All heads turned to watch as the foo fighter took off up into the sky and disappeared into the distance in the span of about three eye blinks. It would be back at Bikini Tower before I finished introductions.

I stepped forward to hug Betty Lou and noticed a man in a uniform bending over to stare at my butt. It's times like these that made me glad I hadn't been wearing a thong when Mr. Doomhilda pulled his Peeping Tom on me.

"Mary Sue, allow me to introduce you to Sheriff Glass. He's in charge of the investigation."

The lawman's gaze shifted toward my cleavage so hard that I couldn't see his face because his brimmed hat covered it.

"Pleasure to meet you but you're wasting your time. We don't need any outsiders to help with our investigation."

"Really? So you think my boobs will be so pertinent to the case that they'll help you find these missing women?"

"What!?" Glass said, startled.

"My boobs. You're examining them with such intensity that I can only assume you think there's some clue in my cleavage that can help you find these women. I'm just curious as to what it would be."

"So you're a smart mouth, are you? Think you can talk to the law like that just because you're famous?"

"No. I think I can talk to you like that because you're being rude and sexually harassing me."

"Well if you don't want me to look at your jugs, then you shouldn't have them hanging out," Glass said.

"My jugs? What a charming and sensitive term to be used by an officer of the law. It's not exactly my choice to dress like this but am I correct in understanding that you would like me to cover up?" My sister looked up at the sky and shook her head. Betty Lou knew what was coming next.

"Why sure. Any gentleman would."

"Am I to assume that you think you're a gentleman?"

"Of course," Glass said with a smirk.

"Well then, a gentleman would offer a lady his coat then, wouldn't he?"

By this point, we had drawn a small crowd of the other people who were on the archaeology dig. A few of them were holding their cell phones out so Glass shrugged and took off his leather sheriff's coat and held it out. "Here you go, little lady. Cover yourself up."

I slipped into the coat and zipped it up. "Happy to. How does it look?"

I spun in a circle.

"Have to admit it looks better on you than it does on me." I pulled the coat down past my hips. The curse takes time to kick in and the length varies but I can always tell right before it happens.

When I felt the magic building, I counted backward from ten. With each number Glass looked more and more confused.

"Zero." At that, the jacket disappeared and I was back to being dressed only in a white bikini.

"What did you do to my coat?"

"Nothing. A witch cursed me a long time ago to always be in a bikini. Anytime I try to cover up, whatever I'm wearing disappears. That's why it's not my choice that my *jugs* are hanging out."

"You owe me a coat."

"And you owe me an apology for leering at my butt and my chest. When I get that, I might consider replacing the coat but not until then."

"That ain't ever gonna happen, so why don't you take your interfering, bikini-wearing bottom and head back to New York," Glass said.

"Not going to happen, Deputy," I said.

"That's Sheriff."

"For now."

"What do you mean by that?"

"Well for one thing, with one post or tweet I can have the media crawling in places you never knew you had." I'm not a huge social media fan but sometimes it's a necessary evil. To be honest, I have Stanley do most of the posting for me under his name of Bikini Assistant. He originally wanted to cut the "istant" off the end, but I put my foot down.

"Tweet all you want. It don't scare me none."

"It should. Especially after I mention how you're bumbling this investigation, not releasing information to the public, and how you don't want a world-class investigator assisting on the case. Then I'll mention your sexual harassment of me which will be backed up by these cell phone videos." I still had on my picture blockers, so I'd be a blurry bunch of lights but the videos would show Glass just fine. "And if I'm not mistaken, next year is an election year for you. I will make it my personal mission to come here and campaign for your opponent. Your small-town sheriff race will become a national story. And may heaven help you if those women are dead when we find them, as I will have no problem blaming it all on you. So if you want to commit career suicide, try to run me out of town. Or accept my assistance in the spirit which it is offered. I will share with your department any pertinent information I uncover. And if I manage to find and rescue the women, I'll make sure to thank you and your department for your assistance in any media interviews I give."

"You're bluffing."

"Bad move, Sheriff. My sister does not bluff," lied Betty Lou. She knew darn well I bluffed when I had to but she knew I wasn't bluffing now.

"Bikini Jones is *your* sister, Dr. Jones?" The Sheriff had his face scrunched up like a chimpanzee trying to understand why people didn't throw their poop.

"We have the same last name. Is it so hard to believe?"

"I suppose it's possible. You must be the older sister then."

I watched as Betty Lou gritted her teeth. "I'm younger. And I'm hiring Bikini as the dig's security consultant so she has every legal right to be on site."

"But not poking around in my county. But seeing as how you made the consequences for doing my job and running you out of town so extreme, I'll allow you to do your investigating so long as you don't cause any trouble and you keep me in the loop."

"Happy to," I said. "How about we start with you sharing all the information you got from the crime scenes."

7

"Were the sheriff's files of any actual use?" Betty Lou said.

"The guy may act like a misogynistic jerk but I can't fault the thoroughness of his work. He managed to collect data from all aspects of the missing women's lives, down to their daily patterns. Problem is, Glass is lacking any actual physical evidence as to what happened to any of them."

"Did they have anything in common? Go to the same goat yoga class, graduate from the same high school, date the same guy?"

I shook my head. "Not as far as I can tell. The only thing they seem to have in common is that they are all unusually beautiful."

"So you think maybe a guy with a thing for beautiful women is behind this?"

"Most guys have a thing for beautiful women but maybe we're dealing with someone who is a bit more obsessive than most. There haven't been any bodies found, no Jane Does in the morgue or the hospitals. In a kidnapping case, anyone missing longer than forty-eight hours is extremely difficult to find. Maybe whoever took them is keeping them alive."

"For what? His own slave harem?" Betty Lou said.

"It's not out of the realm of possibility and it's not as uncommon as I'd like it to be." Human trafficking on Earth and elsewhere was an abomination.

"So what do we do next?"

"What you mean we, Sis? I'm going to go see if I can find any clues about what may have happened to them. I think you have a dig to attend to."

"Oh no, you don't. You're not shutting me out of another mystery."

"Are you still holding onto that grudge? You were fourteen, and I was dealing with necromancer mobsters who not only killed their enemies but then recruited them into the mob. It wasn't safe."

"But that didn't stop me from helping you anyway."

"If by helping you mean getting taken captive and being used as bait to lure me in, then sure, you helped."

"If it wasn't for me, you never would've found their hideout."

"If it wasn't for you, I also never would've been buried in that grave for twelve hours as I struggled to dig my way out with my fingernails."

"Seems like I'm not the only one holding a grudge."

I sighed. "Despite all the grief you give me, you're still my sister and I care about you. I don't want anything to happen to you."

"But it's perfectly okay for you to go off dealing with all sorts of creatures, monsters, and aliens? Why? Because you ticked off Mrs. Doomhilda?"

"Her bikini curse only affected my body. My mind has always been my own."

"I'm not a kid anymore and I'm going to help you find Jenny whether you want me to or not."

I sighed. "You can give me all the information you have. You don't need to come along."

"So, you're going to just take what you need from me then toss me aside like you did Snazzy?"

"You're *still* mad about your teddy bear?"

"*My* teddy bear which you stole and destroyed for no good reason."

"I used it to distract a twenty-foot-tall mutated baby that was about to throw a bus full of nuns over a cliff. It was your teddy bear or forty nuns and their driver. It wasn't that hard a choice."

"But the baby ended up eating and swallowing Snazzy. Grandma gave that to me on the day I was born. You never even replaced it."

"Why would I when you kept yelling at me that no bear would ever be the same as Snazzy and that you didn't want another one?"

"You still could've tried. I mean, you had fought dead mobsters and giant mutated babies. How hard would've been to track down a lookalike bear?"

"I didn't think it meant that much to you or I would've. I took you at your word. I'm sorry."

"Sorry doesn't cut it. And if you're really sorry, you'd let me help." Betty Lou crossed her arms over her chest and glared at me. "If you don't, I'll tell Dad."

"Really? You're claiming to be a grown woman who isn't a kid anymore yet you're threatening to tattle on me." I knew my sister. This argument could go on for weeks and it would distract from my investigation. "Fine, you can come but you do what I say. Remember, you're my sidekick." I took a little more pleasure in that comment than I should have because I knew how much it'd bother Betty Lou.

"I'm not your sidekick! I'm your sister!"

"Sure, if that helps you get through the night."

8

Nine-tenths of investigative work is drudgery and boredom until you figure out how the clues fit together.

I didn't find any major piece of evidence the police missed. No witnesses to the crime. The women disappeared in the wee hours of the morning when they were alone–one on a run, another in her bedroom. One woman was practicing tai chi in the park before sunrise. A cocktail waitress walked out to her car but never made it. Someone had turned the bar security cameras toward the wall so there was no footage. Jenny was sleeping alone in her tent. Yes, there were hotels but Jenny was a hardcore archeologist and preferred a tent. There were no fingerprints on the flap or inside the tent that didn't belong to somebody working on the dig. There were plenty of tire tracks, which all crossed over each other, making any real effort at differentiating tracks useless.

Now, most people would be reasonable when told this. Betty Lou has only rarely been accused of being reasonable.

"You can't find a clue? I thought you were good at this detective thing," Betty Lou said.

"I am."

"But you're stumped?"

I nodded. "Only for the moment."

"What? Do you think a clue is simply going to drop out of the sky?" Betty Lou said.

"It wouldn't be unheard of." And then a crow landed in the dirt near the rear of the pyramid, maybe trying to get a worm. And then I noticed the area around the crow.

"When your team takes something out of the opening in the front of the pyramid, you don't drag it around to the back, right?"

"Of course not. We wouldn't want any damage to come to the artifacts so no dragging, period. And we don't have any reason to go to the back. The entrance is in the front."

"That's what I figured. Can you explain to me why the patch of dirt there looks like someone dragged something through it then pulled a broom behind them?"

Betty Lou went over and the crow cawed at her, looking annoyed. Sis bent down on one knee and examined the dirt. "You're right. It does look like someone's wiped away footprints with a broom but none of my team would've done that. Also, the dragged path leads to the back of the pyramid."

"What's there?"

"False entries, most likely filled with boobytraps to dissuade would-be tomb robbers and treasure hunters. Couldn't fool me though. Sadly, Miskatonic University hasn't approved opening up that side yet. Too afraid of the death traps killing someone and upping their insurance rates."

We followed the path, and it led to an area of the wall that was just a little too out of sync with the surrounding blocks. It looked like a secret entrance which made it way too obvious. I agreed with Betty Lou. It was probably boobytrapped. Oddly, the path went fifty feet to the right of that.

"I think we're going to have to find the back door that path leads to and open it."

"Weren't you listening? Miskatonic University hasn't approved that yet. I could lose my job," Betty Lou said.

"You might, but they can't fire me. If you go back

now, it ensures you have no knowledge of what I'm about to do." I could see my sister having an inner struggle. She's always been the one more likely to follow rules. Rules were important to her. They were important to me too but mainly so I could figure out a way around them or how to break them, so long as I had a good reason.

"No. Something in there may be linked to Jenny's disappearance. You'd have a better shot of getting past the traps with me helping you."

"That's the spirit, Sis. And if Miskatonic does fire you, you can always come work for me."

"Hell, no. I'd work in a fast-food restaurant before I'd work for you."

"Noted. And yes."

"Yes, what?"

I grinned and walked past her toward the wall. "I would like fries with that."

9

Betty Lou kicked dirt in my direction then joined me at the wall of stone blocks and the less obvious door.

"All right, Betty Lou, you're the expert. What's the best way to find and open it and still keep breathing?"

Without a word, my sister placed her hands along the wall of the pyramid and began feeling the stone.

"There's a slight difference in the surface of the stone right around here. Too slight to see, but I can feel it." Betty Lou outlined a rectangle. "The dirt out here isn't disturbed other than the wiped path so my guess is this door opens inward or slides up or down."

"How do we open it?"

"Excellent question. Egyptian Pyramids were built over a wide span and different methods for entry were used throughout."

"You've been exploring the main chambers, so when was this one built?"

"That's the confusing part. By what we've been able to find, it was built for Zoser, the uncle of the first pharaoh that we know had a pyramid."

"Wait, wasn't Zoser the name of that first pharaoh?"

"Yes and no. Zoser was a term of honor for him. Also known as Djoser, but his real name was Netjerykhet. The name was taken in honor of his uncle who left Egypt. We have no idea why, only that he was considered a hero to the people. Zoser's final fate was unknown until we found his tomb here. And here's the odd thing."

"Odder than finding out an Egyptian pyramid was built in North America?"

"Yep. Finding out that the *first* Egyptian pyramid was built outside of Philadelphia. Netjerykhet's pyramid was built around forty-seven hundred years ago, but Zoser's seems to predate it by decades."

"That's huge."

"Exactly. Rewrites everything we know."

"So what you're saying is all bets are off and anything's possible," I said.

"I don't know about anything. I doubt this is an accordion-style door."

"So how do we get the door open? Puzzle? Sunlight refracted through a jewel? Sledgehammer?" That last one got me a look of horror from my sister.

Betty Lou removed a false stone. "This looks like one that opens with sunlight from a certain angle." She looked at the sky. "I'd say the sun will be in place shortly after dawn. We found several jewels in the main chambers. If we start testing now, we should be able to determine if any of them would work in time for sunrise."

"Or we could improvise and save a lot of time." I took the flashlight off my sister's belt. "How many lumens is this?"

"Thirty-two hundred, five thousand, or nine thousand lumens, depending on the setting."

"Sunlight is about ten thousand lumens. Let's hope the people who built this thing don't mind it being off by a bit."

I shone the beam through the pencil size opening. A second later the stone walls started to move, folding in on each other until there was a small doorway.

I chuckled. "Looks like accordion doors it is."

"And of course, you point out that I was wrong. That's just like you," Betty Lou whined.

"Oh, come on. It was funny. What are the odds of

accordion stone doors? And you were being flippant with your answer anyway, so you're partially to blame that it came back to bite you. You want me to go in first?"

"No. This is one of *my* fields of expertise. I'll do it but stay close to me."

Betty Lou and I had to stoop to get through the low opening. Sis reached back and plucked the flashlight from my hand and shone it inside. It wasn't a very big opening or tunnel. There were no hieroglyphics or markings, but it had a dull sheen to it.

"Did the Egyptians use aluminum in their pyramids?" I said.

Betty Lou had her brows creased and was deep in thought but took the time to answer. "No."

"So why is this tunnel made from it?"

"I have no idea," Betty Lou said.

At the end of the metal tunnel, it reverted to a more traditional stone structure.

Betty Lou and I looked at each other.

"Filled with lots of traps?"

My sister nodded. "Undoubtedly. How do we decide who goes first?"

Betty Lou annoys the life out of me most of the time, but she is my sister, and I do love her. She's far more capable than any average person. However, ever since the witch cursed me, being average is something I can't lay claim to. I had the better chance of getting through safely but if I tried to tell Sis that, she'd go off on a rant about how I don't believe in her or some such nonsense.

"Rock, paper, scissor, lizard, Spock, laser, club?"

I shook my head. "How about we just flip a coin?"

"And by *we* you mean *me*," Betty Lou said.

I shrugged. "No pockets in this outfit." At least not

this time around.

Betty Lou rolled her eyes and searched through her pockets. With her suitably distracted, I went into the chamber, stepping on stones that the dust seemed to have been disturbed on. I shouted back, "Heads I win, tails you lose."

"Mary Sue!

"I know you're mad Sis but use the stones I step on and follow behind me."

"Duh! This isn't my first death chamber, you know!"

When I got to the center, it didn't look like any of the tiles had been disturbed. However, one of the tiles was depressed a few millimeters below the rest. Either it was faulty workmanship or an obvious plant like the other door outside. Once, when I was in an Aztec pyramid, fighting off a swarm of winged serpents and spidercats, I encountered the same thing. That time I surmised that someone had already walked through, and the stone didn't pop back up fully. Stepping on it triggered the traps. I wasn't going to fall for that one again so I stepped on the tile next to it.

I guess Aztecs and Egyptians thought differently because that was the wrong tile. Metal guns popped out of Eyes of Ra on the wall and fired laser beams.

I would have been sliced in half if Betty Lou hadn't tackled me from behind and knocked me to the ground.

"Great going, Mary Sue! Maybe next time you'll wise up and let me be the expert with any pyramids traps."

"With an attitude like that, maybe I just will. Now I know you're the expert, but I'm hardly an amateur in these situations. Correct me if I'm wrong, but the ancient Egyptians didn't have lasers, did they?"

"They did not. You know what this means?"

"Time travel, aliens, parallel Earth. Probably at

least a half dozen more possibilities," I suggested.

"The transported Egyptians had help with this pyramid! If I can figure out who, I'll be more famous than Howard Carter."

"Who?" I teased.

"The archaeologist who found King Tutankhamun's tomb." I snickered. "But you knew that. You're just messing with me."

"It's my job as your big sister. However, if Zoser and his cronies had the technology to make laser guns, why didn't they motorize them so they could sweep the room? What's to stop us from just crawling out of here?"

Betty Lou grimaced as we both heard the scuttling of hundreds of tiny little legs. "I wish you hadn't said that."

Between us and the end of the chamber, there were dozens of venomous creepy crawlies headed our way, each bigger than my hand.

"Leiurus quinquestriatus!" Betty Lou whispered.

"Deathstalker scorpions!"

"Duh, I just sent that," Betty Lou nagged. "Don't you have some scorpion repellent?"

"Don't you?" I said and tore off my bikini top.

Most people would wonder why I was getting naked at a time like this. I wasn't. Not exactly and Betty Lou knew that.

While most of the time I don't have pockets, what I do have is a bikini. Mrs. Doomhilda's curse made sure that a new bikini appeared on me in a matter of moments once I took one fully off. I found long ago that with a lot of concentration and focus, I could control what the new bikini looked like. In this case, what appeared on me was mirrored metal with a clasp in the front and the back.

I rolled so my back was to Betty Lou and she undid the rear clasps as I opened the front and we each took a cup.

Betty Lou ran her fingers over the material. "Are you sure this is not just going to be burned through?"

I shook my head as another mirror surfaced bikini top replaced the first on my chest. "Nope. Only one way to find out."

I lifted my hand in front of the flesh searing beam and the laser reflected downwards off the bikini into the swarm of scorpions to fry the leader. I then turned the mirrored cup to cook another.

Betty Lou followed my lead and was knocking the deathstalkers off with the aim of a sharpshooter. Sis had always loved video games as a kid. It was one thing she could consistently kick my butt at.

I handed Betty Lou my cup.

"Hold them off for a minute while I double our firepower."

Betty Lou was reflecting lasers with both hands using two separate beams, the deathstalkers still moved toward us over the burned bodies of their comrades. The chamber was filled with the scent of fried scorpion. In all honesty, it's not a bad delicacy, especially with some garlic, curry, and lemon juice.

I took my latest bikini off and separated the cups so I had one in each hand like Sis and rejoined the great arachnoid cookoff.

"Bet I get more of them than you do," Betty Lou bragged as she picked them off with deadly accuracy while I did more of a sweep with the beam, stopping when I hit something.

"You've got a pretty significant head start on me, Sis."

Betty Lou smirked. "Chicken."

"Fine, but just remember you asked for it. Usual stakes?"

"Sounds good to me."

I stopped and tied one bikini cup on my right foot and then the other on my left and pulled off the third mirrored bikini that had appeared and placed the new cups on my hands. I'd be getting mirrored bikinis until I focused enough to change the template. Now I didn't need to be as accurate as my sister. I just swept the other side of the room with four laser beams back and forth. The first pass typically wounded the scorpions but consequent laser sweeps would finish off the deathstalkers.

"No fair. You're cheating! Like you always do," Betty Lou whined.

"It's not cheating. You never put any limitations or restrictions on how the deathstalkers could be killed."

"But you can redirect twice as many laser beams as me."

"You're welcome to take the mirrored bikini top I'm wearing off me and use that. Then we'd be even."

Betty Lou made the same face she does whenever Mom or Dad tried to make her eat broccoli. "Ick. You want me to take your bikini off you? That's a little freaky, don't you think?"

"Not for some people. I had one website offer me five million dollars to let a couple of women continually undress me as the bikini's popped back on."

"You didn't do it, I hope?"

"Of course not. Can you imagine me trying to explain that to Dad?"

"I'd pay to see that conversation, but you'd have to pay me more than a million to be topless on a web show. Or strip off my sister's top," Betty Lou said.

Now was my turn to smirk. "Chicken."

Neither of us could let that line pass. It was a family personality flaw.

Betty Lou gritted her teeth, crawled over to me, and snapped the front clasp open.

"Come on. Rollover on your side or the stomach so I can pull it off your arms."

The deathstalker scorpions kept coming, apparently well trained enough that the threat of death by laser beam didn't make them scurry away. I pulled one arm down and shimmied out of the strap with my left arm and then repeated the process with my right.

"Mary Sue, freeze!"

Three deathstalkers had managed to sneak around and were two feet from the back of my head.

Oh crap.

Betty Lou shone her tactical level flashlight at the deathstalkers and pushed me away. Fun fact–scorpions are said to be able to sense light not just with their eyes but through their bodies. Normal scorpions would have run away. These three just paused before shrugging it off and moving forward.

By pushing me away, Betty Lou had ended up closer to the deathstalkers. I couldn't use the lasers without risking hitting her too. I took off my boot and tossed it, managing to hit all three scorpions and knocking them back and away from Betty Lou.

"Strike!" I yelled.

"Three is hardly a strike. Maybe a spare," Betty Lou said.

I turned back to see the other scorpions had used our distraction as an opportunity to move nearer. We'd killed more than half but the other half was fifteen feet away. If they got closer than five, we wouldn't be able to angle the lasers to hit them.

"Betty Lou, pick up the spare on those three with

the lasers. I'll focus on their friends."

For once, she didn't argue.

I swept the wave in front as Sis took out the three sneaks.

"Mary Sue, there are more coming through a hole in the wall behind us."

"Well, blast them," I said.

"Really? What an amazing idea! I thought I just sit back and watch their parade as they came to kill us."

The two of us lay on our backs using our hands and feet like we were each some sort of bizarre insect.

Turns out by using her feet, Betty Lou lost accuracy with her hands, so she gave up and just used her arms.

My sweeping strategy continued to work and after what seemed like an eternity, there were no more moving scorpions in the chamber.

"Looks like I win," I said

"Only by two." Everybody in my family has the freaky ability to keep count of ridiculous numbers and do impressive math in our heads. "Let's get moving."

"We've got to come back through here so I think we should clear the laser turrets first," I said. "Then we can just walk."

I didn't think it wise to crawl over so many deathstalkers–a tail could accidentally sting us or one that is almost dead could do it on purpose.

Betty Lou used the mirrored bikini cups on her hands and blasted two laser turrets with reflected beams. "Bet I get more than you do."

"I bet you do too." I used both my hands to focus beams on a turret, again using the sweep method until the beams got there and I held them until the turret was destroyed. The method left laser gouges in the stone walls.

"So you won't compete with me?" Betty Lou took

out another two turrets in the time it took me to fry one.

I took out another. "Oh no. I'll compete, but I concede you'll probably win. Doesn't mean I won't try."

Betty Lou won by seven. For the last two, we both held a mirrored bikini cup in front of the laser so the beam reflected directly back and they blew themselves up.

"I win."

"Congrats," I said. Betty Lou didn't argue when I went first into the darkness ahead of us.

10

It seems whoever built this pyramid didn't have a Plan C if the scorpions and lasers failed and we reached the final chamber without triggering any more traps. There were seven broken clay pots with fluid surrounding the shards. I picked up a piece and sniffed the clay. "It smells like embalming fluid."

"But that doesn't make any sense. The Egyptians mummified. They didn't use embalming fluid. There are hieroglyphics on the jars. Help me piece one back together."

We were both always good at jigsaw puzzles and it only took us a few minutes to rebuild one of the pots.

My hieroglyphic skills were minimal, but even I knew the first symbol meant danger.

"It's in the older style but I think I've got a translation– it says, '*Horrible danger inside. Do not release the monster within. Keep away from women*,'" Betty Lou said.

"That's a little sexist."

Betty Lou shook her head. "No. It means the danger is greater for women. This shows a creature with a huge head, one eye, large teeth, and tentacles crawling into a woman's belly and then bursting forth from her head."

I looked closer at the hieroglyphics. "It's a little faded but I'm not sure that's their stomach the creatures are crawling into."

"It's right over their umbilicus."

"Betty Lou, you can just say belly button."

"I used the proper name," she said. "This might explain what happened to the women. There are seven broken jars, but Jenny was only the fifth woman taken." Betty Lou frowned and looked at the bottom piece.

"That means these things aren't done yet. They still need two more women."

"The next step is obvious, then. I use myself as bait to draw these things out so we can stop them."

"Why do you get to be bait? You think because they only go after unusually beautiful women that they'd go after you instead of me? You don't think I'm pretty enough to be bait?" Betty Lou said.

I fought not to roll my eyes. "It's going to be dangerous and I have more experience with this kind of thing. Plus, I don't want anything to happen to you."

"So it's okay if something happens to you, is that it? I don't see why I can't be bait."

A deep male voice unexpectedly rang out from behind us. "I don't see why you *both* can't be bait."

11

The sudden appearance made us both jump, but only Betty Lou shrieked.

"Sheriff Glass, what are you doing here?" Betty Lou said.

"My office received an anonymous tip that someone was breaking into the pyramid. When I arrived, I looked for you, Dr. Jones but you were nowhere to be found. After some investigation, I find the remains of World War III including blown up sci-fi guns, a ridiculous number of metallic bra cups, and a herd of fried scorpions. What exactly is going on here?"

Betty Lou gave him the rundown.

"I can't let you ladies risk yourselves. You're civilians. Let one of my deputies do it," Glass said.

"Sheriff, you only have two deputies, and both of them are male. Who exactly is going to be the bait?" Betty Lou asked.

"Thompson is twenty-five. He still young and if we put him in a dress, he'll probably make a pretty good looking female. Once he shaves the mustache of course."

"Spend a lot of time picturing your fellow officers dressed as women, do you?" I asked.

"Listen, Bikini, I agreed to your little investigation because you blackmailed me, but this still *my* town. It's my job to protect the people here. If these creatures took five women, I'm going to be the one to stop them."

Maybe the sheriff wasn't a total jerk after all. "I can respect that, Sheriff. How about instead of us working at odds, we pool our resources?"

Glass narrowed his eyes and stared at me, probably trying to intimidate me but I'd stared down a basilisk so he was hardly scary.

"And how exactly do you propose to do that, Bikini?"

"We go ahead with our plan for us to be bait…"

Betty Lou jumped up and down and clapped twice. "Us?"

"Us… but Betty Lou, you are going to do everything I tell you to do."

"And you two will do everything *I* tell you. This will be an official operation of the Sheriff's Department. I'll let you be bait but me and my deputies will be nearby watching everything. At the first sign of danger, the two of you head out and we move in. I'm not going to give in on that, so you can either accept my terms or get out of my county."

"Sheriff, I think I can work with that as long as you're willing to take some suggestions from me," I said.

"And me." Betty Lou was never one to be left out if she could help it.

"I can allow that. But no media circus. Just good solid police work."

I nodded. "Deal."

12

"This is stupid," Betty Lou grumbled.

"I'm sorry Dr. Jones, but how many years' experience do you have as a police officer?" came the sheriff's voice through the earpieces we each wore. "Each of the women who disappeared was last seen near a deserted area."

"I get that but who in their right mind goes into a town park at eleven at night by themselves to sit on a park bench?" Betty Lou griped.

"It's a favorite spot for teenagers to get some alone time or drink some beer," the sheriff replied through the earpiece.

"But I am neither drinking beer nor getting any alone time with anyone. As far as our kidnappers know, I'm by myself."

"Well if it is those things from your pyramid, it's quite possible they'll be a little unclear on human customs," Glass said.

"And if it's not them and it's a person?" Betty Lou asked.

"You've got the county's finest surrounding the park on three sides." The Sheriff and his deputies were covering the park's trio of entrances. I wasn't crazy about Betty Lou being bait but she insisted and it would be less likely for who or whatever was responsible for this attack to try a snatch if they saw two of us. "And you have the famous Bikini Jones looking out for you from atop a nearby tree. Stop yapping and look alone and helpless and read your dang book."

"And that's another thing." Betty Lou appeared to be arguing with her book. "Who comes out to the park in darkness to read a book under a streetlight? It would make more sense for me to be texting on my phone."

"And if it's a human perp, they'd be a bit more hesitant to come at you if they think you might snap a picture or call 911. Now start acting like a victim and try to maintain radio silence unless you see something or need assistance," Glass ordered.

We sat in silence for about an hour.

"All right, I'm bored," Betty Lou said.

"Dr. Jones, just keep reading your book," Glass barked over the radio.

"I already finished it."

"You've been sitting there for about an hour. That book was at least three hundred pages," the sheriff said incredulously.

"Four hundred and thirty-two. What can I say? I read fast."

"Betty Lou, for the most part, stakeouts are long and boring until they're not. Just read the book again," I said.

"It wasn't good enough to justify a second reading."

"Then calculate pi to as many digits as you can in your head." It's something my dad used to make us do on long car trips.

"I already said I was bored. Why would I want it to get worse?"

"Dr. Jones, we're trying to either get your friend back or catch the SOB who killed her. Surely that must be enough for you to put up with being bored for a few hours, wouldn't you agree?" Glass asked.

I heard Sis grumble under her breath but she whispered, "Fine."

We sat watching nothing happen until it was coming up on one in the morning.

"I can't take this anymore. Mary Sue, you got my back?"

"Even on your most annoying day," I replied.

"Then I'm going to pretend to fall asleep. Can't get much more helpless than a woman asleep on a park bench in the wee hours of the morning."

"I wouldn't recommend that, Dr. Jones. Despite all of us keeping watch, you may be the first one to see our perp coming."

"Sorry, Sheriff. I've never been good at sitting still and doing nothing. Besides anyone who gets past you will be spotted by my sister."

Betty Lou started to yawn and stretch out. She lay the book open on her chest and let her head drop down as if she was fighting off sleep but then a few minutes later she closed her eyes and looked to all the world like she was asleep. I knew she wasn't because my sister snored like a freight train and she was quiet.

Nothing happened for over half an hour and then a most frightening sound stole the quiet from the night.

The earpiece squawked with static. "What in blazes is that noise? Are one of those creatures you're worried about attacking?

"No, Sheriff. My sister has *actually* fallen asleep. That sound is her snoring."

"It's terrible. I've heard more pleasant chain saws."

I had to stifle a chuckle which is when I noticed something glittering in a tree at the far end of the park. Whatever it was it was very quiet and didn't even disturb the leaves as it went by. The only reason I noticed something is I happened to be looking that way where the branches were illuminated by one of the park streetlights. "Sheriff, I think we have incoming."

Earpieces crackled with static again. "A man? A woman?"

"Negative. I'm not sure what it is but I don't think it's human. It's in the trees on the west side of the park.

The little I glimpsed looked like either a huge snake or tentacle." Personally, I was hoping for the snake. Even the big ones tend to be easier to fight than things with tentacles. However, the hieroglyphics on the pot showed tentacles, not serpents, so I readied myself.

I was so intent on looking out for my sister that I neglected to watch my own back. I figured I was safe since I was leaning up against the trunk of the tree, but I was wrong.

Something snaked around from the other side, took hold of my elbow, and yanked me off my perch.

I grabbed hold of the tip of the tentacle so it twisted and bent, hard and fast. Something on the other side of the tree trunk shrieked in pain, but let go, dropping me. As I plummeted down, I reached out for a branch and caught it, but it was too thin to support my weight and it snapped. It did slow my momentum so that I managed to land in a crouch and transfer my momentum into a roll.

I got up quickly. It didn't seem like I had injured anything, although sometimes you don't know until the next morning, long after the adrenaline has worn off.

The thing behind me in the tree slithered off the end of a branch but instead of falling, it was floating. I hate telekinetics.

"Sheriff, more than one of those things is here. You and your deputies make sure none of them get out of the park."

"What do they look like?" the sheriff asked.

"Trust me, you'll know when you see it," I said. "They look just like their pictures."

The thing did look pretty much like the hieroglyphics. One huge bulbous head larger than my torso. It had a huge single eye bigger than my head and a mess of tentacles swaying down below it. It had a mouth wide enough mouth to fit a human head, maybe even a pair of shoulders, inside its maw and enough teeth to decapitate someone. Before the stakeout, I'd picked up my travel kit and changed my bikini. Now it was red and the bottom had a holster that I filled with a neural disruptor. It looks like a sci-fi ray gun and shoots out energy bursts which can stun pretty much anything with a nervous system. I'd also left my camera blockers behind. To some beings, infrared would make me as easy for them to spot as if I was waving a flashlight.

I took a shot at one that had floated across the park and was about to enter into tentacle grabbing range of my sister. When the energy hit it, the creature convulsed and dropped to the ground.

Amazingly, it wasn't knocked out but began crawling towards Betty Lou. I turned and fired at the one dropping towards me but before I could pull the trigger again, it used its telekinesis to yank my neural blaster out of my hand, then throw me to the dirt.

As I turned to scramble away, it floated up behind me and grabbed me with two tentacles on either arm and one on my legs.

I didn't know if it was telepathic and had read my thoughts or just had an idea that biting off human heads sounded like fun, but it pulled me toward rows of teeth that would make a megalodon shark envious. I struggled but couldn't get free of the creature's grip.

"Hey buddy, watch the tentacles. I mean, I can understand your attraction. I'm a beautiful human woman. On the other limb, you're a cyclopean, tentacled creature. It would never work out between us. Now put me down and surrender quietly and I won't have to kick your ass. Or whatever similar anatomy you have for me to kick." I've found that making quips and talking tough always helps in a fight where I am outmatched.

Sometimes it serves as a distraction. Other times it can make my opponent lose their cool, but most of the time it was a stalling tactic to buy me enough time to figure out what to do next.

Tall, green, and grabby wasn't inclined towards making conversation. It did pause and look at me as if it was just realizing I was talking to it. My struggles to get out of its tentacled grip brought it out of contemplating its equivalent of a naval, or umbilicus as my sister would say, and restarted my journey towards decapitation.

Inches from becoming this thing's late dinner or early breakfast, a book flew past my head to nail the creature in its eye.

It let go of my right shoulder to raise that tentacle towards its pupil. I used the distraction to twist the tentacle between my legs and bite the one on my left shoulder. The thing's grip loosened enough for me to squirm free and fall to the ground. I scrambled towards the fallen neural blaster but I got there too late.

Betty Lou had already picked up the ray gun. She pulled the trigger and fired twice, knocking the second creature from the sky.

It was down but not out. I was impressed that the thing could still move. In fact, a tentacle reached up and grabbed my wrist.

There was something different in the grip this time. Before it had been brutal and practically savage. Now its touch was almost tender. Looking up with its one huge eye, it spoke for the first time.

"Betty Lou, Bikini, get out of here. They're coming and they want your brains too."

"Who's coming? Why do they want our brains? And how do you know our names?" Betty Lou peppered the cephalopod with questions before realization finally dawned on her. "Jenny?"

The creature nodded her bulbous head and made a sniffling sound although I couldn't see anything that remotely resembled nostrils or a nose.

The creature that was Jenny moved sluggishly, as if each motion was an extreme effort.

"The sheriff..."

Betty Lou nodded. "We called him in already. He's outside the park. Don't you worry–we'll figure this out. Bikini's an expert on weirdness and saving people. If anyone can fix this, my sister can."

That was probably the nicest thing my sister ever said about me in my presence.

The bulbous head shook side-to-side. "Run away from...."

Speaking proved too much for the altered Jenny and she couldn't finish her sentence. I saw movement. As I looked up, three more airborne tentacled big heads floated toward us, one from the front and two from behind. I tried to lift Monster Jenny. It wasn't happening.

"Jenny, can you move so we can get you out of here? You're too heavy for us to lift," I said.

The bulbous head again moved side-to-side. Her answer sucked and severely limited our options. There weren't enough shots left in the disrupter to take down the other three and if they housed the missing women's brains, killing them wasn't an option.

Neither was us dying.

"We gotta go," I said, grabbing Betty Lou's hand.

"What about Jenny? We can't just leave her here," Betty Lou whined.

"There's nothing we can do to help her right now. But don't worry, Jenny. We're coming back for you." I had to drag my sister away. She finally ran as she saw one of the cephalopods floated far ahead of us along the path we were running on.

Betty Lou fired the neural blaster at the one in front of us.

"Betty Lou, no!" I shouted too late. She turned and fired a pair of shots at the ones hovering behind us. None of the blasts reached their targets.

"They're still coming!"

"That's because the neural blaster is a short-range weapon. You're too far away to hit them," I said.

"No problem. I'll just wait until they get closer and shoot again."

"No, you won't."

Betty Lou gave me her most exasperated look. "Are you kidding me? Even in a situation like this, you are going to give me grief because I got the gun and saved you? Just because I want to shoot the rest of them and you don't want me to? How petty are you?"

"It's not about being petty. The blaster only holds six shots. You just wasted the last three." As if she didn't believe me, Betty Lou pointed the gun at the one in front of us and pulled the trigger again. Nothing happened.

"Oh, poo." I guess it was a tribute to our parents that even in a time like this Betty Lou found herself unable to curse. "Put in a new magazine of stunner shots."

"That's not how it works. It runs on a battery that takes over a week to charge off a special generator. That thing's no more helpful at this point than a paperweight."

"What are we going to do then?"

I went to the nearest tree and broke off two large branches and tossed one to my sister.

"Anything we have to."

"So you want me to fight off floating, cyclopean, cephalopod monsters with a stick?"

"You could use your bare hands but the stick gives you a little more reach," I said.

Betty Lou sighed. "I always knew you'd be the death

of me."

"I'm here because you called me, not the other way around. And I seem to *distinctly* remember asking you not to come."

"Fair point. Any advice on the best way to hit them with a stick?"

"The ends of the tentacles are sensitive but hitting them there is unlikely do much damage. I'd say go for the middle of their eyes."

Betty Lou's pupils got wide. "What if they have the brains of the missing women?"

"The Quid survived for centuries in a pot in a pyramid. I seriously doubt we'll be able to do them much harm." I might be able to kill at least one but that would destroy the woman inside. Better to fall back and regroup and bring in more weapons from the tower. "We just want to disable them long enough to get away. And Jenny didn't speak to us until after the neural blast which tells me that something else is in control here, not the missing women. The blaster blocked that control. At least temporarily."

The floating cephalopods moved at a lazy pace as if they realized we weren't going to be able to get away from them and they were taking their time.

"Why aren't they attacking?"

I shrugged. "Maybe they don't want to hurt us because they want to turn us into those things."

"Einstein's boxer shorts! That ain't happening." Betty Lou charged the lowest floating cephalopod and jabbed her branch at it. In response, it did two things. It rose, and both branches were yanked away as if by invisible hands then floated above our reach.

"If it can do that to the branches, why aren't they doing it to us?" Betty Lou said.

"Maybe it's telekinesis doesn't work on organic

material," I offered.

Even a time like this, Betty Lou had to point out my flaws. "But the branches are organic."

"Maybe they can't use it on living things."

"But you just broke those branches off. They could still be grafted onto another tree so they're not exactly dead."

"What I do is not an exact science. I make my best guess, go with it, improvise a lot, and do my best not to die. Maybe there's a weight limit and we're too heavy."

"That at least makes sense. Although technically they are levitating themselves, which means they are able to lift a living thing and they're bigger than we are. And you couldn't lift the one with Jenny in it so they're heavier than us," Betty Lou said.

"It could be a combination of tasks. Concentrating to make themselves float may limit what else they can do," I said, exasperated, trying to figure a way out. Arguing over stupid picky details wasn't helping.

"Okay, I can accept that one."

"I'm so glad," I said.

"So what's the plan?"

"I'm still working on it," I said as we moved back to back and spun, trying to keep all three of the airborne creatures in sight.

"Work faster," Betty Lou shouted.

"Like you yelling that at me is going to help make it happen."

"You don't have to get so cranky about it. I'm just trying to help."

I had to stop myself from punching Betty Lou in the arm like we did when we were kids. "How is nagging me to hurry up going to help in any way?"

"I figured since you always like to show me up, a little encouragement would push things along," Betty

Lou sneered.

"Nagging and encouragement are two different things, Sis," I pointed out.

"All you do is complain."

The sound of a siren along with red and blue bubble lights flashing made the creatures turn from us as Sheriff Glass's patrol car burst into the field alongside us.

"Get in!" Glass shouted through an open passenger window of his patrol card. "That is if you two can stop arguing long enough to be rescued."

Betty Lou threw open the back door of the police car and we both rushed in. I slammed the car door behind us.

"Go!" Betty Lou screamed.

The Sheriff's car peeled out, throwing up dirt and grass. I looked behind us. The floating creatures were following but couldn't keep pace.

When we got to the edge of the lawn, Glass hit the brakes and put the car in park. We were surrounded on two sides by trees.

"Why are you stopping?" Betty said.

"Sheriff, this is lousy cover."

"It'll do."

"No, it won't!" Betty Lou screamed. "We need to get away and come back later with reinforcements. Or at least, Bikini with some heavy weaponry."

The Sheriff turned around to look at us through the wire mesh of the police car that would normally serve to protect the cops from bad guys in the back. "Because I really don't want that to happen."

"What? Why not?" Betty Lou said.

The Sheriff pointed the barrel of a gun through a gap in the mesh. "You'll find out soon enough."

I recognized the weapon - it wasn't a traditional

gun. The turncoat lawman pulled the trigger. There was a whoosh of air as a dart flew towards Betty Lou. I managed to reach out and snatch it before it hit her neck.

I just wasn't fast enough to catch the second dart that embedded itself in my shoulder.

The tranquilizer began to work almost instantly. My eyelids felt like lead and the world went blurry. My limbs felt a hundred times heavier, like I was moving through oatmeal.

I threw myself over Betty Lou but Glass still managed to land a dart into the side of her neck as my entire world faded to black.

13

"Not again."

I would've understood had I been the one to say that. I'd woke on a surgical table. My wrists and my ankle were bound by sturdy rope to the corners. My phone, watch, and boots were gone. The knots seemed solid and there were a lot of them. I looked over to see that Betty Lou was in the same predicament. Actually, she was in a similar situation but not quite the same. Betty Lou was now dressed in some sort of toga lingerie in addition to being tied down to her surgical table. Oddly enough, her glasses had been left on and her hair was still in a bun.

The place didn't look right for an operating room. That's because it wasn't. It was the autopsy area in a morgue, probably the one used by the county.

Betty Lou saw me and glared back. "What? You're the only one in the family who can have adventures?"

I raised an eyebrow and didn't say a word.

"Fine. An old boyfriend asked me if it would be okay if he tied me up. I agreed, not realizing he would do it in the middle of the night while I was sleeping."

"Impressive, Dr. Jones," Glass leered. "I would never have taken you for the adventurous type. In fact, I never would've thought of taking you at all, except for a matter of convenience. But having spent more time with you, I realized you are quite a beauty. I have no idea why you choose to cover it up by wearing such conservative clothes."

"I don't dress for you, Sheriff. And what in blazes are you doing? Why are you in league with these creatures?"

"That's quite a long story but I suppose you have the time since you're not going anywhere. The Quid came to Earth many, many centuries ago. It took all the forces of ancient Egypt to defeat just seven of them. But even their best sorcerers and warriors only succeeded in reverting the Quid back to their larval state by removing part of their brains. Which is why the man who could have been Pharaoh chose instead to protect his people and traveled across the Atlantic Ocean. He ended up in North America in an attempt to get the Quid as far away from his homeland as he could. He built this, the first pyramid, and then had it buried with him when he died. The fool thought that his mummy would awaken to stop the Quid if they ever got free. Goes to show you that some people can be smart in one area and idiots in another."

"You mean like you?" Betty Lou said. "Bikini's people know where she is. Your deputies heard everything on the stakeout."

"See, there you go, proving my point. A woman like yourself who is so brilliant in the field of archaeology and quantum physics still thinks that my deputies will be coming to save you."

"You mean they're in on it too?"

"No, Sis. It means they were never there to begin with."

"Very good, Bikini. You get a gold star."

"What kind of misbegotten, pathetic, reprehensible, and odious excuse for a man are you?"

"The kind that's finally getting what's coming to him," Glass said.

"You are going to get what's coming, but it's not going to be what you think," I promised.

In a situation like this, it's best to keep your captor talking. Monologuing is even better. Besides giving you a chance to figure out how to escape, most of them are so proud of their little schemes that they can't help but tell you all the details. The bigger the ego, the longer the speech.

"So how exactly did you even know that these Quid were in the pyramid? You don't strike me as the type to be able to translate an ancient book written in hieroglyphics."

"You're right there, Bikini. It was nothing so mundane. These higher beings choose me as their prophet and spoke to me in my dreams. At first, I assumed it was just sort of indigestion causing me to have these weird nightmares but after a couple of months, I realized that they were trying to communicate with me. Once Dr. Jones's team unearthed the rest of the pyramid, it was a simple matter really to sneak past her meager security to rescue the Quid from their prison."

"How'd you get past all the traps?" I said.

"No big deal. They put the blueprints in my mind, and I was able to get in and out without any difficulty. It seems the brother and uncle of the pharaohs had used magic, mummifying techniques, and the Quid's own weapons to lobotomize these beautiful beings. By taking away part of their brains, he shrunk them down to their child forms, so weak that some simple fluid could hold them trapped for millennia. I freed them, and they told me that they could use human brains to replace what was taken in ancient Egypt. If I helped them, they could return to their former glory."

"Why women?" Betty Lou asked, catching on about keeping him talking. So far, his knots and the ropes were holding.

"Not all that complicated. Larval Quid are able to phase through matter briefly. By going through a woman's womb, they can pass through the rest of her easily and remove the part of the brain that they need. They leave the rest of the body intact."

"What difference does that make? Without a brain, the person will die anyway," Betty Lou said.

Glass stood up and stroked Betty Lou's cheek. Sis tried to bite his finger off.

"So feisty," the sheriff said. "And you note I didn't say they took the whole brain. They leave this Sherry Balla and a few other parts."

"You mean the cerebellum?" I said.

Glass shrugged and walked towards the foot of our morgue tables. "Sure, that's probably it."

I didn't understand people like this sheriff. "How could you betray your badge? You're a cop, sworn to protect and serve."

Glass leaned his head back and laughed. "Sure, but what has it ever gotten me besides a paycheck? I'm forty-four years old, divorced, and haven't had a date with a good-looking woman since high school. Thanks to the Quid that's no longer an issue. Now I have a harem."

Glass turned towards the morgue door. "Oh ladies, come in here." One by one, the five missing women filed in past the body coolers to stand around the sheriff. Each one of them was dressed in some sort of skimpy outfit. Glass wrapped his arms around the shoulders of two. They moved with all the animation of robots as they shifted closer to him.

"The Quid leave behind enough of a brain for the women to walk and listen to commands..."

"But they can't even talk to you. They can only do what you tell them to," Betty Lou said.

"I'm okay with that. Conversation is overrated."

"You're deranged!"

"Yeah, but I'm happy. How many people can say that?"

"And how many people can say they sold out humanity so cheaply?" I asked.

"Not that cheaply. Not only do I get a harem but when they take over the world, I get to be Emperor of New Jersey. And let's be honest. There are lots of people who would have done the same thing."

"But there's many more who would never even consider it," Betty Lou said.

"Dr. Jones, you're just deluding yourself. But that's okay." Two larval Quids, each smaller than a basketball, scurried on tentacles up each of the morgue tables. One stopped to stand between my feet, the other between Betty Lou's. "It won't be long now before you two become the final members of my harem."

"Oh, snickerdoodle!" It was a testament to our parents that even with an alien larval monster about to enter her womb and steal her brain that my sister still couldn't bring herself to use a stronger curse.

Then she started babbling what sounded like ancient Egyptian, but I wasn't paying attention. Instead, I was using techniques I learned from Darcy Dhodinna, the world's greatest escape artist, to get free. I managed to dislocate one of my ankles and a hand to slip out of the bonds. I drop-kicked the larval alien that was creeping slowly up the table so it smashed into Glass' face.

I tore off my bikini top and the next one that appeared had razor-sharp edges for shoulder straps. I put my ankle and wrist back into the joints. It hurt like hell but I used meditative techniques taught to me by the Ninja Clown Monks of Newark to numb the pain. I used the saw straps to cut the other ropes until all my limbs were free. I quickly cut through the rope on my sister's left hand and gave her the razor-edged bikini top and grabbed the larval Quid that was already past her knees. I grabbed it, but it grabbed onto my sister's toga. I threw it into an opened body cooler and it took most of the filmy fabric with it.

The other tiny brainnapper had crawled off the sheriff's face and was creeping back toward me. I grabbed a tentacle, tossed the larva into the same cooler and slammed the door, then spun back in time to see Glass get to his feet.

"Ladies, form a human shield," he ordered the functionally lobotomized women, and they obeyed. "My Quid Masters, come quickly!"

I didn't want to hurt the women's bodies. I knew several techniques that would render then unconscious–although some may not work without a full brain to affect–rather than killing them. The problem was that Glass had pulled his gun and I couldn't disarm him without hurting at least one of the women.

He waited as the Quid floated toward the morgue door.

I recognized the one with Jenny's brain and the other one that had been stunned. Each of them held onto the frame with a tentacle as they passed. They seemed unsteady as they floated. The pair seemed to get stuck and take up the entire doorframe, blocking the rest of the Quid from coming in.

Glass trained his gun on me. "Bikini, stay still and I'll make this as painless as possible."

I ran and hid behind the body coolers.

Glass fired his service revolver at me over the shoulder of one of the brain-limited women. The shot hit the metal cooler wall, inches from my face.

"You shoot me and I won't be suitable for your harem," I said.

"It would be a pity, but better to lose you than to have you stop us. And I owe you for making my jacket disappear. I loved that jacket."

Glass pointed the gun at Betty Lou, who had both hands free and was working on doing the same for her legs.

"Surrender or I'll shoot your sister."

"No, you won't." I managed to get a hold of an autopsy scalpel. Now I just needed an opening to throw it into the sheriff's jugular. "You already admitted she was hot."

"I *do* so like the idea of making the uptight Dr. Jones do some very nasty things. I would far rather have her than you, Bikini, so I guess you're right. I won't shoot her. Yet. But there are others who while lovely don't hold the thrill of your sister. I guess I'll have to cull one of this delectable herd if you don't surrender." Glass turned his revolver on one of the zombified women's heads and it was one I knew.

"How much do you care about your friend Jenny? She's only basic hot so if I have to sacrifice her to get Dr. Jones, I can live with that. Drop the scalpel and step out or I'll blow what's left of Jenny's brains out."

What else could I do? I dropped the scalpel and put my hands up which made Glass laugh as he pointed the gun directly at me and pulled the trigger.

14

I yanked open the body cooler door. and it took the bullet meant for me.

Glass cowered behind his shield of lobotomized women and fired again. I was moving before he pulled the trigger and the bullet missed. I turned toward the traitorous lawman hoping to get the gun before he got off another shot.

It didn't work. I was still three feet away from Glass when he fired. I was too close to dodge. Reflexively, I lifted my arms in a feeble attempt to stop the bullet.

I heard the shot, but there wasn't any pain. I wasn't dead or even wounded, but it wasn't due to any effort on my part. I was alive because someone else had gotten in the bullet's way. Jenny's lobotomized form spun, positioning her between me and the gun. The bullet tore through her throat and her remaining gray and white matter.

Shocked by the sudden movement of one of his slave harem, Glass froze long enough for me to grab hold of the barrel of his revolver and ram the palm of my hand up into his nose.

Blood spurted from his nostrils as the sheriff collapsed to the ground next to the woman he had just killed. I had his gun in my hand and had to stop myself from putting a slug between Glass's eyes. Killing a defeated opponent was not the Bikini way.

I turned towards the Quid with my friend's brain.

"Jenny, are you in control in there?"

The bulbous head nodded. In a voice that sounded like nothing human, she said, "I have been ever since Betty Lou hit me with the ray gun. Same with Susan over there who you blasted. Even though I'm disconnected from my body, I was still able to exert some control. I was trying to save you and grab his gun but it didn't work out like I planned. Am I dead?"

My two eyes met her huge one. "Your human body is. I'm so sorry. Thank you for saving me."

Jenny the monster nodded and a huge mouse drowning-sized tear fell. "We've got to get you two out of here before the three of them get through." The other Quid had given up on pushing their way through the door and their tentacles were smashing little holes in the wall instead.

"Is there another way out of here without going past the rest of the Quid?" I said. Like most morgues, this one was underground, with no windows or doors that I could see.

"You have the Sheriff's gun. Could you shoot them?"

"No. If we use a neural disrupter, the rest of the victims can take control of their host bodies. If we hurt the Quid, we hurt the women whose brains are trapped inside."

Then a huge smile crossed my face.

I donned a pair of long surgical gloves. Anything below the elbows or the knees didn't disappear when I put it on which was good because I'd hate to walk around in bare feet all the time.

There was a container on a shelf full of embalming fluid that held a human heart. I took the metal top off the glass jar and use a pair of medical tongs to lay the heart on the surgical table.

I filled a large syringe with the embalming fluid but it had no needle. It was used mainly to suck up bodily fluids, not inject anything.

"Betty Lou, you almost done back there?"

Just as I spoke, she finished slicing through the last

rope on her ankle.

"I'm free, but I'm not exactly ready to go anywhere. That larva thing shredded my clothes." Sis was holding bits of fabric over her important bits. "Is there anything in here I can wear?"

"No idea, but we need to get out of here."

"I'm not going anywhere naked. There has to be a lab coat or something around here to wear."

Clutching the fabric shreds to her, Betty Lou checked but there were no lab coats or scrubs. She even checked the body freezers that didn't contain the larva Quid. All the human bodies were naked.

"You could always take one of their sheets and make another toga out of it," I said.

"I'm not wearing a sheet that's been on a dead person."

The smirk appeared practically of its own accord. I'd been waiting for something like this to happen for years. "There is one other option."

Betty Lou understood right away. "There's no way I'm wearing one of your cast-off bikinis."

"Why? You've got the body to pull it off," came the screechy yet gravelly voice of Jenny the Quid.

"It's a bikini or a toga made from a dead person's cover sheet. Or you can just streak through the town if you prefer."

Betty Lou let out a growl of frustration. "Fine."

I stripped off my latest top and bottom then tossed them to her. Another one materialized in less than ten seconds.

"Why's it so heavy?"

"After I took off the bladed one, I focused on making the next one Kevlar. I figured it wouldn't hurt." The one that materialized on me was made from the same stuff.

"This thing is too small. And don't you dare say I'm

too fat," she said.

"I would never call you or anybody fat. People are beautiful regardless of their shapes." It's a shame so many people are too superficial to realize that. "And you're not fat, you just have curves. You look great."

Betty Lou finished putting the bathing suit on and brushed it off like she was cleaning dust off a suit. She took a deep breath and stood up straighter. "Thank you."

I picked the scalpel up from where I dropped it. Then I pulled more ammo off the bad sheriff's gun belt and reloaded the revolver before handing it to my sister. I picked the syringe off the table then opened the cadaver drawer back a couple of inches and squirted the contents of the syringe inside.

Both larval Quid screeched, so I threw open the metal freezer door and grabbed the closest larva with both gloved hands. I slammed the door shut with my hips.

Even hurt by the embalming fluid, the larval creature was trying to grab my hands with its small tentacles and bite me with its many tiny teeth. I raced across the room then dropped it in the embalming fluid and put the lid on tight.

The larval Quid went instantly catatonic. I picked up the jar with my left arm and held it close. I held out my right hand toward Betty Lou.

"Give me the gun, Sis."

"Why do you get the gun? Why can't you get the scalpel?"

"Because I'm planning on pulling the same trick that the sheriff did. I'm going to point this gun at this thing and tell them to let us go or I'll pull the trigger and kill the larva."

"What's to stop them from using telekinesis to pull the gun away?" Betty Lou said.

"The fact that you're going to tie it to my hand with that surgical thread over there and then do the same with the jar. Then fill up some more syringes with embalming fluid from that other jar. They might come in handy."

For once, Betty Lou didn't argue. She found five more syringes and filled all of them. "Now what?"

"We see if they care enough about each other to back off and let us pass."

"And if they don't?"

"I shoot this thing and we fight our way out."

"Great." Betty Lou furrowed her brow and looked at me as if she was disappointed. "But isn't that kind of mean? Shooting a baby?"

"It's not a baby. It's a devolved alien creature bent on stealing a woman's brain so it can try to take over the world, not to mention kill anyone that gets in its way."

"Good point." Betty Lou found the scalpel cover and put it on before putting the blade in her bikini bottom waistband and held the syringes in her hands. "I assume these will do more damage than the scalpel."

I nodded. "Jenny, we're ready to go."

Jenny the Quid nodded her bulbous head and looked at the Quid next to her in the doorway. "Susan, float aside and let them in."

Susan the Quid floated to one side and Jenny to the other. The first of the three other brainnappers squeezed through the doorway and floated towards me and Sis. "Stop right there. You come any closer and I put a bullet in junior's head."

They didn't respond in English but in a series of guttural cracks and whistles.

"Jenny, did you understand any of that?" I asked.

Jenny the Quid's huge head nodded. "I can access this thing's memories. They threatened to disembowel you if you hurt the little one."

"You're welcome to try, ugly." Before I'd finished, an unseen force tried to pull the jar and gun way, but Betty Lou's knots held.

"Stop it now or I'll shoot."

The telekinetic tendrils vanished, and both items were under my control again.

"Now let all four of us pass and do not try to stop us."

There were more guttural squeaks and clicks.

Jenny translated. "He said that you must be simple in the mind because you are unable to count. There's only two of you and their lackey, the sheriff, would only make three."

"You can keep that scumbag. I mean us." I pointed my nose at my sister then at Jenny and Susan the Quids.

"What about our bodies?" came the high-pitched squealing yet guttural voice of Susan the Quid.

"Glass is not going to let anything happen to his little slave harem. He only has four left. We'll rescue them later. We need to get you both out of here before they figure a way to transfer control back to the brainnappers you are sharing bodies with."

The center floating Quid made more unpleasant noises.

"He said you'll never get away with this and you will die a very painful death."

"I hear that a lot but I'm still here. What's it going to be?"

The other two Quid floated in the door and then over by the cadaver drawers.

More guttural clicks and squeals.

"He says you won't be able to get away," Jenny translated.

"Come after us at your own peril."

Susan the Quid and Jenny the Quid exited first,

followed by Betty Lou. I backed out after them. I shut the morgue door with my feet and Betty Lou jammed a mop stick in the two handles. I stopped only for a brief look through the window. One of the Quid had used its tentacles to raise Glass by the ankles and was shaking him awake.

We ran for the exit. Well, Betty Lou and I did. Jenny and Susan floated.

15

Sis and I ran onto the deserted street treading carefully since neither of us had shoes.

"We need to find someplace defensible that they can't get through. And we need weapons. If we can get to a phone, I can call my office and have someone bring reinforcements and neural blasters," I said.

Betty Lou grinned. "The weapons would be good, but I already called for reinforcements."

"When did you do that? Never mind. Give me the cell phone you used."

"I didn't use a phone."

"And how did you call? Smoke signals?"

Before my sister could answer, tentacles ripped the front door off of the police station and threw it at us. Jenny caught it with her tentacles and threw it back. It went wide as the full Quid had better aim than the archaeologist in an alien body.

"I'd hoped we would've gotten further before they got out." Although honestly, it shouldn't take a telekinetic that long to pull a mop away from a pair of doors.

Glass' face was a deep crimson with blue veins popping up from his forehead to his neck. "You dumb whores would have been smarter to join my harem. We're going to kill you dead!"

"Exactly how would you kill us living?" Betty Lou shot back.

"Drop the little Quid, and maybe we'll make it quick."

Before we could tell the crooked lawman to go to hell, Jenny the Quid was soaring through the air, low enough that her tentacles were undulating along the ground and pushing her down the street much faster than I had seen any of the others move.

In seconds, she was on top of the evil sheriff.

"You did this to me. You killed my body!" Jenny the Quid screeched.

"Ending up in there is your fault for turning me down when I asked you out on a date. As for your body getting shot, I didn't want that to happen. I wasn't done with it yet but that's what you get for not listening to me, your master."

There is a rhythmic gurgling that sounded like it might be laughter. "You're not my master." Quid Jenny then used her tentacles to pull both Glass' arms apart like he was a wishbone. Even from where I was, I heard the pops of his shoulders as they dislocated.

Glass' alien masters didn't care too much about him because they didn't even try to save him. Instead, they floated towards us. The scalpel shot out from where Betty Lou had tucked it in her bikini. The plastic blade cover flew off and then it shot towards my jugular. Susan the Quid reached out a tentacle to catch it but with little experience moving tentacles, it ended up stabbing into her instead. Her screams were the sounds of nightmare.

"I wasn't joking. If you attack again, this one is dead." For effect, I tapped the gun barrel on the glass jar.

The evil Quid must not have believed me because a rock flew through the air but not at me. It shattered a storefront window into pieces and the glass shards floated up then sped toward us.

I pulled the trigger and put a bullet in the larval Quid's head and shook the remains of the jar off my fingers. I had some minor cuts from the bullet shattering the glass, but the larval Quid wasn't moving.

I had five bullets left in the gun but they were useless against a swarm of glass.

The shards seemed to be ignoring Susan the Quid. Probably didn't want to hurt their own, assuming they'd get control back. Instead, the shards flew towards Betty Lou and me.

Susan placed her tentacles on her bulbous head as if concentrating. The Swarm of glass slowed.

She wouldn't be able to hold off long against more experience telekinetics. I turned, grabbed Betty Lou's hand, and pulled her toward a car.

"Trunk!"

Sis nodded, and I used one bullet to shatter the window of the car. I reached inside to open the door and pulled the latch on the driver's side floor to pop the lid. Betty Lou jumped in. I leaped in after her and slammed the trunk down.

It was just in time. We heard the glass shattering into smaller fragments as it battered the car like a deadly tinkling rain.

16

Betty Lou was controlling her breathing which meant she was fighting hard not to show she was freaking out. "How long should we stay in here?"

"I don't know. It's not safe to get out now, but if we stay here too long, they'll get us anyway. Maybe we could figure a way to get the trunk lid off and use it as a shield."

The attack stopped and there were a bunch of guttural clicks and squeals and a sizzled impact.

I wanted to pop the lid to see what was happening. "That sounded like a magic blast."

"Oh good. That means my reinforcements have arrived," Betty Lou said.

"I still don't get how you could call for reinforcements without a phone."

"You're not the only Jones who can think fast on her feet. Did you hear what I said while I was getting loose from the ropes?"

"It sounded like ancient Egyptian, but I'm hardly fluent. I figured you didn't want to disappoint Mom or Dad by cursing in English, so you did it in a language they didn't speak."

"Good guess but completely wrong. Remember when I told you I made sure I deactivated the curse so the mummy wouldn't awaken?"

"Yeah."

"Those were the words to turn it back on. Now that I know that Zoser's purpose was to keep those things in check, I knew he'd track the brainnappers down. The only reason they were able to contact Glass to help them escape was because I deactivated the curse in the first place."

"Good thinking, Sis," I said.

"You don't have to sound so surprised when you say it."

I popped open the trunk. and there was indeed a mummy attacking the three evil Quid with a long golden staff.

"It looks like his staff has the Eye of Horus," I said.

"No, it's the Eye of Ra, which was on Horus's right eye and therefore that common confusion. It's a powerful, destructive force linked with the heat of the sun. The original eye was the manifestation of Wadjet, the daughter of Ra whom he sent down…"

"TMI, Sis." Although it did explain the golden blasts that resembled sun fire shooting out of the staff that knocked a Quid out of the sky.

The other two Quid managed to telekinetically pull the staff out of the mummy's hands before flipping it over and impaling Zoser in the chest.

"Idiots," Betty Lou and I said in unison. Anyone who has ever fought a mummy knows all their organs are kept in jars and stabbing them in the chest won't do anything but make a big hole.

The Quid that had been blasted by the magic staff was lying on the ground and crawling away, using its tentacles to drag its huge body.

"Help me!" it screeched and clicked in English.

The magic staff seemed to have the same effect as the neural disruptor. The woman had control of the Quid body.

"We need to convince Zoser to blast the others or let us do it," I said.

"So you know how to operate the Ra-rod?" Betty Lou said.

"Sounds like something we would use when we were cheerleaders. Not exactly, but it's been my experience that given enough time I can figure most things out."

"Given my expertise, I can probably figure it out in half the time," Betty Lou said.

"Fine. You go pull it out of the mummy's chest and use it."

Sis shrugged. "I was hoping you might be able to get it, then give it to me."

"Of course, you were."

The Quid nearest the mummy swept Zoser up in its tentacles and bit his bandaged head off.

"Ouch," I said.

Betty Lou straightened her glasses. "It's a little better attack than a chest wound but the mummy body should still be able to operate since its being run by a spirit not a brain," Betty Lou said.

At that point, my plan was just to get the Ra-rod out of the mummy's chest rather than convincing Zoser to work with us. Depending on the strength of the spirit possessing the mummy they can be intelligent or dumb as a stone. Don't get me started on their anger issues. Yes, being in a preserved body for centuries isn't a picnic but don't take it out on people who had nothing to do with your predicament.

I had to change my plan when the Quid bit down again to sever the mummy from the waist up and swallowed the rest of his top half, including the staff.

"How are we going to get the Ra-rod now?" Betty Lou said.

"So it's we now? You're going to help?"

My sister shrugged. "Depending on what's involved, I might."

Gingerly, I climbed out of the side of the trunk to avoid cutting my bare feet on any of the glass on the ground. Betty Lou followed. I turned back and pulled out a gas can and a rubber tube, then handed Sis the gun

I had untied.

"Go to the driver's seat and pop open the gas lid, then tie this on your hand."

"Why?"

"Because the gas cap is the key to stopping the Quid."

"Really?" she said.

"No. I need the gas. Go."

Betty Lou popped the lid and took off the gas cap and stuck the tube in.

"Are you going to set them on fire? Won't that damage the women's brains?"

"No, I'm not going to set them on fire." I bent down on one knee put the tube in my mouth and sucked the gas up like it was a straw. A bit got in my mouth. I bent over, spit it out, gagged, and almost retched. I put the outside end of the tube in the can and drained the fuel.

Betty Lou smiled when she finally caught on. "You're going to make it regurgitate Zoser's pieces."

"Exactly." I pulled a syringe out of my sister's waistband.

The gas can filled quickly. Not bothering to put the lid on, I grabbed the can and ran towards the Quid that was munching on Zoser.

I closed the distance. When it opened its mouth to take another bite out of the bandaged body, I flung the gas can in its maw. It hit a few teeth, but I made the shot, and the can went down its throat.

The other evil Quid floated a rock towards another window so I pushed the plunger. I got great distance. The squirt stream went over twenty feet and nailed it in the eye. It seemed to burn it like acid, making the Quid's huge eyelid close and the rock dropped to the ground.

There was retching from the Quid who'd been enjoying the all you can eat mummy snack bar. A moment later, the pieces of the mummy came pouring out along with some of the foulest smelling vomit I've ever encountered–and I've been inside more than one monster's digestive tract–along with the remains of a pizza and a bowling ball.

I held my breath, so the smell didn't make me throw up as I put a foot on the mummy's chest and wrapped my hands around the magic staff.

"Sorry about this," I said just in case the mummy was the kind that had full awareness and I pulled hard on the Ra-rod. With all the foul digestive juices, it was hardly as regal as the time I pulled Excalibur out of a meteor, but it got the job done.

Betty Lou was waving at me to bring her the Ra-rod, but she was still back by the car.

The mummy-eating Quid recovered from its tummy ache faster than I'd anticipated. Its tentacles wrapped around my waist and lifted me off the ground. I ignored it in favor of examining the staff. It looked like a basic mystic biosensor. If I was right, I just had to put my index finger on one side and my thumb on the other, then squeeze.

I had a clear shot at the Quid who was not trying to eat me so I blasted it first. Big mistake. Sure, it fell to the ground, but that only made the mummy-eating Quid pull me towards its open mouth even faster.

17

Spinning the golden staff in front of me, I held it up so the Quid bit down on it instead of me. Despite the danger of being eaten or losing an arm, I didn't let go.

I had planned to squeeze the trigger sensor but my hand slipped down the staff and I couldn't reach. I tried to bring my other hand in to pull me back up but it didn't help. I leaned back and flipped so my ankles were above my head and scissored the Ra-rod between my feet and squeezed.

That got me a great big nothing. The Quid dragged me down, so I tried to hold on with my toes. It didn't stop me but I managed to activate the trigger and a golden blast of sun fire magic went right up into the roof of the Quid's giant mouth and it fell from the sky.

Unfortunately, I was still beneath it.

In vain, I fought to lift an alien that weighed as much as a rhino high enough for me to crawl out. Luckily, the woman whose brain was in the Quid had taken control and rose up on her tentacles, freeing me.

She spit out the staff and asked me in grunty and squeaky English. "Are you all right?"

Struggling to my feet, I did a quick once over. The right number of limbs, no sharp pains. "Nothing broken, I think."

Betty Lou ran up to me. "We did it! We freed all the women's minds from the aliens' control."

I couldn't help but smirk. "I don't see this as much of a *we* effort."

"Hey! I got one with the neural blaster disruptor."

"The mummy got one too. I got three."

Betty Lou shook her head at me. "It always has to be about you, doesn't it?"

"Which upsets you because you think you should be the center of attention," I countered.

"How would I know? With you around, I've never been."

Jenny floated over to us. "Neither of you has anything to complain about compared to those around you."

I felt ashamed, and Betty Lou's cheeks flushed.

Back where she'd been, Sheriff Glass was beaten and battered, but still breathing.

Susan the Quid floated our way too. "Are we stuck like this forever?"

"Will the Quid be able to take control away from us again?" asked one of the other women trapped in a brainnapper's body.

"I don't know the answer to either of those questions for sure but I have a plan to restore your brains to your bodies," I announced.

Jenny the Quid's huge maw of a mouth frowned. "But my body was killed."

I nodded and reached my hand up to where the shoulder would be if tentacles had that joint. "I know. My plans may not be able to help you, but I may be able to make sure you keep control of *that* body."

"I don't know if I want to live life as a monster," Jenny wept.

"You could never be a monster," Betty Lou said. "You're one of the nicest, sweetest, smartest people I know. And look at all the advantages you have now. You've got all those limbs to uncover artifacts, and you can use your telekinesis to get things out of the ground a hundred times faster."

"But my boyfriend is never going to want to go out with me again. We've only been dating for three months, and I really like him."

"You're probably right about that but don't give up on dating entirely. There are a lot of men who are willing to overlook a lot of things and get turned on by aliens," I said.

"Seriously?"

I nodded. "Women too. They have conventions and lots of aliens go to them just to get lucky with kinky humans."

"Might be interesting, maybe something I'll have to check out."

"Um, guys?" Susan the Quid pointed with one of her tentacles behind us. "Is *that* going to be a problem?"

The mummy's torso had pulled itself over to where his head had landed and was placing it back on his neck. The bandages moved like writhing snakes and fashioned the head onto the body while the legs rolled their way to the torso, those bandages reaching out to pull those limbs back together with the body.

"Maybe. Sis, any chance you could redo your curse deactivation?" I said.

Betty Lou shook her head. "It doesn't work that way."

"Should we attack him before he attacks us?" Susan the Quid asked.

"No. Fighting is rarely the best response." Although sometimes it is the only one available. "Let me try to reason with him first."

I held out my hand to my sides, as it was the best way to place the Ra-rod behind me and out of sight. No sense in showing off that I stole his staff.

"We've eliminated the threat of the Quid. I now want to save the women whose brains they stole."

Zoser wasn't having any of it and lunged at me. IA quick spin and a clownkido move added to his momentum, so he landed on his flat on his face on the pavement, his feet up in the air like a pratfall.

"Let me handle this, Mary Sue." Betty Lou spoke to the mummy in ancient Egyptian.

Zoser got up but didn't charge my sister. Instead, he responded in the same language. The two of them held a civil conversation for several minutes.

Finally, Betty Lou turned to me. "He says he will give you until when the sun sets tonight to try to save the women whose bodies yet live. He insists that you prove that you can remove the Quid's control from Jenny completely and that she won't be a danger."

I looked at my watch. It was four-thirty in the morning. The sun was going to set in a little over fourteen hours. "Thank you."

"And he wants the Ra-rod back."

I hesitated. It was a dangerous weapon, but technically so was Jenny. How could I ask him to trust me if I couldn't do the same? I handed the staff to Betty Lou who gave it to Zoser the mummy.

"I have to make a phone call if we have any hope of making this happen."

In minutes, my Saturn shuttle was headed our way with Hany at the controls.

18

I decided to approach the apartment from the outside, not wanting to blow Dr. Dendrite's cover. I slid down from the roof along the fire escape as silent as any clown ninja had ever been. Imagine my surprise to find a dog sitting on the fire escape and smoking.

"You know tobacco is no good for you, even in a pipe," I said.

The dog took a long drag on the pipe and then blew out the smoke in a ring.

"I'm aware, but I also genetically engineered my own tobacco to get rid of most of the harmful effects. While it's not safe, the risk is reduced. Unfortunately, it's still very addicting, even if it's just to my brain. Plus, the pipe helps me think. And I get a break."

"Trouble in doggy paradise, *Mr. Cuddles*?"

The dog shrugged. "Not so much trouble as needing a few moments to myself. Harper is a wonderful child but my brain is that of a 50-year-old man. Sometimes I need a minute alone to commune with my thoughts. I suspect that moment is ruined."

"Why's that?"

"I very much doubt you're here for a social visit, Bikini. If you were here to spy on me to make sure I was doing what I said, I probably would never have seen you."

"True enough. I have a favor to ask."

"You're hardly in any position to ask me for any favors."

"I saved you from the Tommy Gunners."

"Bah. I would've gotten away from those simpletons

in short order."

"I didn't tell Harper that you could talk. Or that you're her father."

"So, it's blackmail now, is it? Who would've thought that Bikini Jones would sink this low," the dog with the human brain said.

"I don't think it will come to that. If you've truly have turned over a new leaf, you'll want to do the favor," I said.

Dr. Dendrite's doggy ears perked up and twitched. A second later the door to the room that led to the fire escape opened.

"Mr. Cuddles! Where are you?" came Harper's voice.

Dr. Dendrite's dog form had a look of utter terror on his furry face, and his tail tucked between his legs. Suddenly the sides of his collar opened up and a pair of thin mechanical attachments telescoped out. One tapped a brick from the wall which opened like a small door while the other one reached up to take the pipe from his mouth and place it in the gap behind the brick. The first mechanical limb closed the brick before they both retracted back into his collar.

"Impressive. Why didn't you use that to get away from the Tommy Gunners?"

"Because I wasn't wearing it. Harper thinks my pink one with the rhinestones looks prettier."

The young girl came to the window. "Mr. Cuddles, are you on the fire escape again?" Harper looked out and saw me next to her dog. "Bikini! What are you doing out here?"

"I came to ask you if I could borrow your dog."

"Why do you need Mr. Cuddles?"

The dog with the human brain rolled his eyes.

"Because she needs a favor from me." My jaw dropped at how casually Dr. Dendrite blew his cover.

"What favor do you need, Bikini?"

I looked between the dog and the little girl and then back again. "She knows you can talk?"

"Of course I do. But we haven't told my mom. Sometimes grown-ups don't believe stories that don't seem normal coming from kids," she said.

"True enough," I agreed. It was a major failing of adults. And her mother was also Dendrite's ex-wife and had banned him from seeing their daughter years ago. I doubt she'd let him stay if she found out.

"What do you need me to do?" doggy Dendrite asked.

I laid everything out. "Aliens took most of the brains–everything above the brainstem–from five women. One of the bodies was killed but the other four are still alive, living on just basic body functions. I need someone to take the brains out of the aliens and put them back in the women. And to find a solution for the woman whose body was killed."

"So you want me to perform four, or maybe even five, brain transplants for no compensation?" Dr. Dendrite said.

"Mr. Cuddles, I'm surprised at you. You're a dog. What do you need money for?" she said.

The dog shrugged. "My dear Harper, it's not always just about money. There are many ways to be compensated."

"True. One of them is just doing a good deed to help people. Think of all the good Bikini has done for the world. She doesn't ask to get paid for all of it," Harper said.

"Still she's rich," Dr. Dendrite said.

"True, but she did it before she got rich, didn't

she? And she would keep helping people even if she didn't have money. How can you not help people who need you?" Harper gave the dog a gander at her own very impressive set of puppy eyes.

And they were working. The so-called Mr. Cuddles was very confused. The doctor didn't seem to know how to respond and looked at me for guidance. I kept my mouth shut for a bit just to make him sweat.

"There would be compensation. You would be a hero to this wonderful young girl here. Can you imagine anything better than that?"

Dr. Dendrite growled and whispered in Greek, "Μπικίνι, παίζεις βρώμικη πισίνα. Αυτό είναι χαμηλό, ακόμα και για εσάς." Which translated as "Bikini, you are playing dirty pool. This is low, even for you."

I smiled and tossed my hair over my shoulder.

I set up the pitch but Harper knocked it over the fence. "Please Mr. Cuddles, be a hero. For me?"

The dog sighed. "Fine, Harper. For you."

I grinned. "Thanks. I have transportation waiting on the roof. I'll bring Mr. Cuddles back to you as soon as I can."

"Bikini, you won't let anything happen to him?"

"Of course not."

The girl picked up the dog then hugged him and kissed his snout. "Mr. Cuddles, you be good and listen to everything Bikini tells you, all right?"

"I'll take it under consideration. Now let's go before I change my mind."

"Wait, Mr. Cuddles. Aren't you going to kiss me goodbye?"

The dog looked at me and rolled his eyes as if embarrassed. Then he licked the little girl on the cheek.

I motioned to the ladder and doggy Dendrite

shook his furry head. "Oh no. I'm not climbing a ladder. You want my help, you carry me."

"Fair enough."

I picked up the dog and climbed up the fire escape to the roof using my feet and my one free hand.

19

"No, I won't do it. I absolutely refuse to play second scalpel to a dog. Especially one who doesn't have the decency to even be a purebred," grumbled the man in surgical scrubs.

"You absolutely will, Dr. Gibson," I said. "I'm your employer and you will do as I tell you."

"Very well. Then I quit."

Dr. Gibson had always been full of himself, thinking because he was a surgeon, he was far above the rest of humanity. I only kept him on the payroll because he was highly skilled and a lot of times the Bikini Relief Team went into disaster areas where we needed someone with his skillset. He could assess an injury better than an MRI machine and perform surgery three times faster than just about any other traditional doctor I've ever seen.

"Okay, Dr. Gibson." The surgeon smiled smugly assuming I was about to beg him not to go. I'm not big on begging. "I'm sorry that you're leaving the Bikini Foundation but I wish you well in your future endeavors. Security will meet you to clean out your belongings. You have ten minutes to vacate the building and turn in your security ID badge."

"That's it? You're firing me?" Gibson stood with his eyebrows raised so high they almost joined his hairline.

"I didn't fire you. You quit rather than help four women regain their lives. I think it's a cowardly move but I understand that you think you're not up to this task of such difficult surgeries."

"Not up to the task!? You know very well that I am ranked the fourth-best surgeon in the world. And the fastest."

"But Dr. Dendrite here was never even considered for that list. He is so far beyond other surgeons that the medical community can't bear to contemplate him among their ranks."

"That is because this *man* put his own brain into machines, mythical creatures, aliens, and now a mangy mutt," Gibson said.

"I freely admit he thinks outside the box, but the success of his work cannot be argued. And to the best of my knowledge, he has never done permanent harm to another person or being. I understand that you're afraid that you'll lose your ranking when it's compared to what he can do. It's perfectly understandable that you don't think you can keep up."

"Not only could I keep up, I'd operate circles around him."

"I admire that you haven't given up your illusions to continue with your trash talk, but that's all it is unless you're willing to put up or shut up. And rather than putting up you decided to run away like a dog with his tail between his legs. From an actual dog. You now have only seven minutes to vacate the building, Doctor."

There was a rumble in Dr. Gibson's throat and he looked over to where Dr. Dendrite the dog was making his preparations for surgery. His mechanical collar now had a pair of human-sized mechanical arms. The canine mad scientist had heard our entire conversation and was grinning, not to mention wagging his tail. He looked up and waved with one of his mechanical arms at the griping surgeon.

"Fine. I'll help the dog but only because those young women need my skills."

"That's quite magnanimous of you, Dr. Gibson. Thank you and I accept the rescission of your resignation."

I walked over to doggy Dendrite.

"Nice job of using Dr. Bighead's ego to manipulate him," Dendrite said. "Just like you used my daughter to manipulate me."

"I'm sure I have no idea what you're talking about," I said in a tone of voice that made it clear that I did. "What's your prognosis for the patients?"

"For the quartet of women with the intact brain stems, it should go well, although I cannot make any guarantees even with the mystically enhanced stem cells you've obtained. There is an element of risk involved in any surgery, even with me and the likes of Dr. Bighead."

"What about Jenny?"

"Therein lies the real problem. I could reanimate her corpse but the bullet destroyed her brainstem beyond any hope of what I could repair or regenerate. If you could provide a donor corpse with an intact brainstem, I could do something. Or another species or being she wishes to be put into."

"I've already discussed this with Jenny. She would feel like she's desecrating a corpse if she took another human body and wouldn't feel right about it. There is no other animal or creature that we have access to that holds any interest for her. I offered the possibility of a robot or mechanical body. When she realized that she would have an almost total loss of sensation from the outside world except for the most basic sensory feedback, Jenny nixed that idea as well. She's gotten used to the Quid body she's in now. It's not ideal and she would much prefer her own but she would be okay staying where she is at. Do you think you could remove the Quid's brain without impairing any physical or mental function? That way we can be sure the Quid won't regain control and make her a slave again or try to take over the world."

Dendrite's mechanical right hand stroked the fur on his doggy chin. "I've looked at the scans. There is a very slight possibility. But I won't know for sure until I get in there. I will need to work around all the neural pathways and made certain I replaced any severed links. I'm going on my best guess on which portions grant the telekinesis but I think I have it worked out. Without the mind power, she'd have a lot of trouble walking and moving in Earth's gravity. I'll run through the plan in my mind while I am performing the other surgeries."

Dr. Gibson sneered. "Don't you think you should be devoting your full attention to the surgery you're doing?"

Doggy Dendrite sneered back. "How cute. I forget that lesser intellects are incapable of focusing on multiple tasks simultaneously. How limiting that must be for you."

"Both of you, play nice. We have five lives to set right. Do either of you need anything else from me?"

Dr. Gibson shook his head.

"You don't have enough time to go to med school so you can assist me in the surgery instead of your colleague here?" Dendrite said.

"I'm afraid not. Plus, it's not a good idea for me to operate on someone as I can't wear scrubs for more than a few seconds. I'll leave you both to your work."

It took them three days to finish all four of the brain transplants. I invited Zoser the mummy to be my guest in Bikini Tower and he observed the first operation from the surgical observatory before his deadline. Betty Lou came as his translator. He was impressed that we could not only take organs out but put them back. Zoser asked if we would be able to put some of *his* organs back in. I told him I didn't know but that we would look into it. In exchange, he extended our deadline and went to the Met to see La Traviata with Betty Lou who was fascinated by the mummy and constantly asking him questions about his native time.

"Isn't asking the same as cheating for an archeologist?" I had asked.

She ignored me and borrowed my car, even though it would have been easier to walk than to drive and find on-street parking–Sis was too cheap to pay for parking.

Meanwhile, Dendrite and Gibson were operating machines. Each of them took maybe an hour to nap between each surgery. Dr. Gibson may not have had Dendrite's genius but by the end of it, I think the mad scientist had developed a begrudging respect for Gibson's skill, perseverance, and endurance.

Since it wasn't an emergency and they would need to be at the top of their game, both doctors slept for about sixteen hours before tackling Jenny's surgery.

20

Dr. Gibson looked over the scans for Jenny's alien body and shook his head. "I don't understand how this creature can have two smaller brains instead of just one big one. What happened to the one it was born with?"

"Zoser told us that before he became a mummy, he and his people had managed to capture the Quid. Their embalmers went in through the mouth and removed the rear brain. The forebrain was too well protected by dense tissue to reach. They were trying to kill them but instead ended up reverting them to their larval state. The hides around their heads were still tougher than their weapons so they were unable to kill the larval Quid, so they placed them in the jars of embalming fluid. The Quid escaped a time or two and were recaptured. It was deemed too dangerous to keep them in Egypt. Along with a small army, Zoser took the dormant larval Quid as far away from his people as he could and ended up outside of Philadelphia which was uninhabited at the time."

"But these Quid aren't even terrestrial in origin. How is it even possible that a human brain is compatible with theirs? How do they overcome rejection?" Gibson said.

"From my limited experience with alien life, I've noted that a great many beings seem to share a similar template, although there are a remarkable number of variations possible within those parameters. The human brain is very resilient and if you're able to revert portions of it to a stem cell state, growing fresh connections to a new host is not terribly difficult. That's how we were able to grow back the neural connections in the four women we've already operated on. Although just to be safe, we're keeping them in an induced coma for two weeks until they heal completely," doggy Dendrite said.

"Which explains why you always disappear for months at a time when you change host bodies," I said.

"Very true. Although the human brain doesn't have pain receptors, it does have the ability to process pain, and no one wants to go through that. It's much easier just to sleep and later wake up new and whole."

"But if what you explained to me is correct…"

"If?" Dendrite said in an insulted tone.

"Then why do the Quid need a second brain if the first one is able to perform the bodily functions?"

"Simple my dear doctor. The larger brain houses most of their telekinetic potential as well as an amazing computational ability. Each of these creatures could function as a computer to calculate everything necessary to navigate a ship between stars or any other tasks they put their minds to. I suspect that's why they only brought seven Quid to conquer the world, even thousands of years ago. If this works, Jenny will only be able to perform a fraction of what a natural Quid could do with the same body. She'll lose some of her telekinetic strength, but it should still be enough for basic levitation and other necessary tasks."

"What are we going to do with the second brain we have to remove?" Dr. Gibson asked.

"For one, I would love to study it, preserving it so it didn't die, although it would retain a portion of the telekinetic abilities, so it would be dangerous if it gained sensory organs and was able to interact with the world. I left that decision to Bikini who feels it's too dangerous so we're going to turn the brain over to Zoser."

"Who?" Gibson asked.

"The mummy. He will be allowed to dispose of it."

"It was part of the deal I had to make for him to accept Jenny keeping the body," I said.

"So Dr. Gibson, are you ready for round five?"

I had expected the surgeon to look fearful or nervous, but instead, he was excited.

"I am."

The pair exchanged grins, and I half expected a fist bump. Or a paw and fist bump.

Even though I wasn't a medical doctor, I have extensive knowledge of terrestrial and extraterrestrial physiology. I sat in the surgical theater looking down as the two men used a mystical scalpel from the lost city of Shangri-La to cut open the Quid's head. We used anesthetic to keep Jenny's brain under and a low-level electric current through the Quid to keep it unconscious.

I'd never actually had the experience of watching Dendrite at work before this week. Even with mechanical arms attached to a dog collar, he was brilliant, moving expertly through the pia and dura mater and the various parts of the alien nervous system. Gibson was going all out but was managing to keep up.

Once Dendrite had severed all the neurological connections and had cauterized the vessels, he used his mechanical arms to remove the Quid's second brain. It was the size of a small beanbag chair with ten times more sulci and gyri–the wrinkles in the tissue–than a human brain had. Instead of white and gray matter, it had green, orange, and yellow varieties.

Dendrite held the alien brain over the containment unit. As his mechanical arms lowered it down, hundreds of web-like strands shot out from the brain and embedded themselves into the ceiling and the walls.

Dendrite shouted out an explanation for what happened but I'd already figured it out. The alien brain had so many neural pathways and enough telekinetic power that it shot out its nerves like razor wires as a protective mechanism.

Dendrite's collar flashed, and the dog was surrounded by a translucent force bubble. Gibson wasn't so lucky. Even without access to eyes, the Quid brain somehow knew exactly where the human surgeon was and retracted a hundred nerve fibers from the ceiling and shot them towards him.

I was already making my way into the surgery room but I wasn't going to be there in time. Dendrite realized this too, so he dropped his force bubble then ran on his four stubby legs. Doggy Dendrite got between Gibson and the alien brain. His mechanical arms reached out and grabbed a gurney and flipped it in front of them as a shield. The nerves were slowed but managed to push through the metal and keep coming.

"Gibson, curl yourself into a ball!"

Instead of arguing with the dog, the human surgeon listened. Dendrite jumped onto the surgeon's side and reactivated his force bubble.

The nerves ricocheted off the field but kept trying to force their way in.

Bikini Tower got attacked on a semi-regular basis. The team and I built defenses into every room and hallway. Before I entered the operating room, I grabbed a full-sized clear body shield and a neural blaster. Hiding behind the shield, I shot at the alien brain. The weapon was on the nonlethal setting for humans. Since we left weapons out for anyone to use in self-defense, I wasn't comfortable providing random people with the means for lethal force.

The blasts made the web of stabbing nerves twitch but didn't seem to do much else. It did manage to turn the creeping nerves away from the doctors but only so they could come after me instead.

The nerves seemed to be learning and instead of shooting straight at me and through the shield, the tiny alien bits slithered around the force field. The first thing they went for is the gun which was what I figured it would do. All the weapons I manufacture have an override built-in just for me. Once it read my DNA, the security safe settings were deactivated, and I ejected the energy magazine as the gun was ripped from my hand. I tried to take the shield with me as I backed away, but the nerve web held it fast.

After grabbing a surgical tray, I dove under Jenny's operating table, hoping the alien brain would hesitate to attack me near a body it hoped to reclaim. Using suture thread, I tied the energy magazine to a syringe with a 7-gauge needle.

The tiny tentacles of nerves blocked my exits on all four sides of the under-table. The tray also held the Shangri-Laian scalpel, so I started slicing. The brain vibrated in the ultrasonic range with what I can only imagine was a shriek of pain. By the sound, Quid brains *did* have pain receptors.

Scrambling out through the gap, I got close to where the alien brain hung, not floating, but suspended on its own nerve fibers. I touched the needle to the scalpel which would give it the same mystic cutting properties for a few seconds, clicked the energy magazine to full overload and launched the syringe at the alien brain. The magically charged large needle stuck in the side of the brain like a dart. Nerve fibers reached out to remove it but weren't fast enough.

The magazine blew, releasing the entire disruptor's energy in one concentrated blast.

The writhing nerves stopped, and the strands drifted flaccidly from their anchored positions throughout the room as the Quid brain plummeted to the floor.

I checked on the surgeons. They were both safe in the force bubble.

"Dr. Gibson, can you close on your own?" I asked.

Dendrite dropped the force bubble and the human surgeon got to his feet. "I… don't know. Maybe."

"Nonsense. Of course, you can, Gibby," doggy Dendrite said. "What a ridiculous question to ask a surgeon of Gibby's caliber."

Gibby shot the canine look of surprise and a nod of thanks.

"Good. Dr. Dendrite, I need you to make a neural disruptor harness for this thing to make sure it does not wake up again."

"Give me thirty minutes."

"You have ten."

"This isn't the *Enterprise* and I'm not Scotty. I might be able to pull off twenty-five but you can't rush quality. You want something quicker or something that will keep this thing from waking up?"

"Fine. Just get it done as fast as humanly…" Dendrite's furry face glared at me. "Or caninely possible, please and thank you."

I used my phone watch to call for a half dozen neural disruptors to be brought into the operating room.

Dendrite had it done in twenty-seven minutes.

21

Zoser the guardian mummy was quite pleased when Jenny, Betty Lou, and I arrived at a large and scary-looking chamber in his pyramid to give him the forebrain of the Quid. He seemed especially happy to see my sister.

Zoser used his staff to examine Jenny the Quid, then turned to Betty Lou who translated his ancient Egyptian when he spoke.

"I thank you for keeping your vow. I can find no trace of the Quid's maleficence left so Jenny shall be allowed to live."

I wasn't about to let him kill Jenny regardless but this was the outcome I wanted so I managed to keep my thoughts to myself. "Thank you. What are you going to do with the brain and the other Quid?"

The mummy spoke again and pointed towards the sun.

Betty Lou watched the mummy with goo-goo eyes and smiled as she translated. "Zoser is going to revert them to larval form. He was wondering if you could send them to Ra."

"I might be able to make that happen. Are you certain there's no chance of rehabilitating them so they won't try to harm people?"

Betty Lou translated his response. "To them, we are less than an insect is to us. What matters the concern of an insect? They will rule and kill without consideration for anything. It is safest for our world if they weren't in it."

"Very well."

"Hello, lawman being held captive against his will

over here. How can you just ignore me?" Glass shouted at us. The traitorous lawman was strung up in his boxer shorts-which were covered in little hearts-and bound upside-down over a pit filled with translucent and glowing phantom crocodiles. At the sound of his voice, one of the ghostly crocodiles leapt up toward his face, making him cringe, then start trembling and whimpering.

It was easy to ignore him, but it wasn't the Bikini way.

"Zoser, I would like you to release Sheriff Glass to me so that he may face human justice," I said.

Betty Lou translated again.

"Glass betrayed humanity, his entire race. One such as he does not deserve life but a long and painful death. By the time the servants of Sobek…" A crocodile-headed Egyptian god. "… are done devouring this filth, even his Ba will be no more."

The Ba was one of the five parts of the soul the ancient Egyptians believed in and the one that held the personality. Destroying it would erase him from existence.

"As fitting a punishment as that may be, we are supposed to be better than someone like him. Justice can be tempered with mercy."

The mummy nodded and Betty Lou translated once more.

"Very well. But only because you are such a noble warrior and brilliant wizard."

Betty Lou smirked when she said the last word. I'd long ago stopped correcting folks from low tech cultures who assumed I had magical powers. Sure, I have mystic artifacts and scientific gadgets, so who's to say that doesn't qualify one as a wizard from another's viewpoint?

Zoser took a blade from a stone block and spun to

throw it at Glass as he stomped on a floor stone. At first, I thought the mummy was killing Glass rather than turn him over to a court of law and prepared to fight him. Then the knife sliced through the rope and a metal ramp shot out below him so he fell and slid to the upper level instead of beside the phantom crocs.

Betty Lou scowled at Glass. "You're going to jail, scumbag."

"For what? Helping aliens steal human brains that you've apparently replaced? Good luck proving that in a court of law. I'm a cop with twenty-five years on the job. I probably won't go to trial. Even if I'm convicted, I'll probably get off with community service."

Jenny lifted Glass by his ankles and dangled the naked lawman in front of her huge mouth and all its sharp teeth. "You're a sick bastard who abused our bodies." Dr. Dendrite had also tweaked her new speaking parts, so she sounded almost human. "There was enough DNA evidence to prove that."

The Sheriff didn't seem scared of the archeologist in an alien body. "So I'll do a few years in minimum security until they parole me."

Betty Lou continued to translate for Zoser.

The mummy moved faster than any centuries-old dead thing should have been able. The ancient Egyptian had his fingers around Glass' throat before any of us could stop him. Zoser flipped the upside-down man right-side-up using his neck, then held Glass above his bandaged head. Jenny grinned with all those teeth and unwound her tentacle from his ankles.

Once more, Zoser spoke in ancient Egyptian.

The sheriff was trembling like a leaf on a tree in a hurricane. "What'd he say?"

"Zoser here just promised that if you ever get out of your human prison that he will personally come to kill you painfully by ripping all of your organs out of your body one by one before feeding your soul to his phantom crocodiles." Betty Lou grimaced. "Personally, I hope you get off scot-free so the mummy makes you pay for what you've done. Even those few years in prison wouldn't be that long to a mummy who has been around since the beginning of recorded history. A real man would face Zoser head-on. A coward like you will probably plead guilty to everything to make sure he never gets out of prison. Pity."

The mummy threw Glass across the chamber. Jenny the Quid floated over and wrapped a tentacle around his feet and dragged the boxer clad Glass out of the pyramid where his own deputies were waiting to arrest him.

Once Glass was out of earshot, I turned to my sister. "My ancient Egyptian is pretty basic, but it sounded to me like Zoser said Glass was lucky the mummy didn't throw him in with the phantom crocodiles."

Betty Lou shrugged then tried and failed to hide a grin. "So I embellished the truth a bit. There is no way somebody like Glass should ever see the light of day outside of prison."

I couldn't agree more.

22

Two weeks passed quickly. All four women were awoken from their induced comas, outwardly none the worse for wear.

We threw them a *You've got your body back* party at Bikini Tower and invited their families and friends. Even Dr. Dendrite and his daughter Harper came, although she still didn't know their actual relationship went beyond that of owner and unusual pet.

Of course, the only one not having a good time was Betty Lou.

"I can't believe Miskatonic University fired Jenny just because she got stuck in an alien body. It's discrimination. We should sue."

"Unfortunately, there is a precedent to support their very wrong decision," I said.

Jenny gently laid a comforting tentacle on my sister's shoulder. "I appreciate you sticking up for me like that but you didn't have to quit."

"Yes, I did! I not going to work for idiots who'd can one of the top archaeologists in the world just because she's acquired a giant head and a bunch of tentacles! You've accomplished more at that dig in the last two weeks than all of us managed in the last two months. They're idiots financially too because you're doing the work of a dozen regular people for the salary of one."

"Now that you're unemployed, you could always take me up on my offer of making you the chief archaeologist for Bikini Enterprises," I said.

"Me? Working for you? I can't think of a worse torment. Besides, I've turned that job down a half dozen times before. What makes you think I'd say yes now?"

"I didn't think you would, but I have always kept it open for just in case you changed your mind. I wanted to offer you one last chance at the position. Since you passed, would you mind if I offered the job to somebody else?"

Betty Lou is a royal pain in my rump but she wasn't stupid. She looked over at Jenny and her one big eye as she floated in the air nearby. Sis smiled. "No, I wouldn't mind."

"Great." I waved Jenny over to join us. "Jenny, I'd like to ask you to come work for me as my chief archaeologist. In the course of doing what I do, I come across plenty of ancient ruins and alien sites that need to be explored and their artifacts cataloged. The job is yours if you want it."

"Salary?"

"Significantly more than you made at Miskatonic U," I said.

Her bulbous head nodded. "Does it come with benefits, especially dental? Because I've got four times as many teeth now as I used to."

"We have in-house doctors and dentists."

"Then sign me up, Bikini."

Jenny wrapped her tentacles around me and hugged, then did the same with Betty Lou. I may give my sister a lot of grief, but I also had to give her a lot of credit. She didn't cringe and her return hug was sincere. Jenny floated over the tell her parents–who were still not quite used to having an alien for a daughter–about her new job.

Now it was time to grill my sister about a more personal matter. "What's this I hear about you dating?"

"How'd you find out about that?"

"Seriously? World-famous adventurer and owner of a Fortune 500 company here. Do you really have to ask? By the way, I love the way you screwed over Miskatonic

University and helped your new boyfriend at the same time."

Betty Lou blushed. "Zoser's not my boyfriend yet. Not technically." Sis chewed on her lip. "So you're okay with me dating a more than four-thousand-year-old mummy?"

"Sis, you're free to date whoever you want. Considering some of the people, including a few who didn't technically qualify under that classification, I've dated, I'm the last one who is going be judgmental. Besides you have a lot in common. Who else can you chat in ancient Egyptian with? How do Mom and Dad feel about you dating a guy who's way older than they are?"

"I figured I'd wait for Thanksgiving before I said anything, just to make sure things are going to work out. Zoser is working with Dr. Dendrite on having his organs put back in, so let's see how that turns out. Besides, now that I put in his claim to the pyramid, the surrounding property, and all artifacts inside, Miskatonic has to return every artifact that was removed by our team and can't keep exploring the premises."

"They mustn't have been happy about that."

"Nope. Too bad for them. That's what they get for firing my friend. Oddly, there are two items they are denying they received. A scroll and a necklace."

"Great. Nobody at Miskatonic University has ever caused any problems with an ancient scroll or book before." My tone went over bordering on sarcastic to taking up residence there.

"Stop being so judgmental. The trustees that encouraged that nonsense are all gone. The ones there now are just your garden variety idiots."

"I'll believe that when the artifacts are returned intact." Although they could simply scan the scroll, then return it. "So Miskatonic is banned but you aren't."

"Exactly.

"I'm proud of you, Sis."

"For sticking up for a friend?"

"That too. I meant how you stepped up with all this Quid business. You impressed me."

"Thanks, Mary Sue. It's nice to hear you finally say that. Any chance you could repeat it for Mom and Dad?"

"Well, I do need to get you something for your birthday next week…"

"You are cheaping out on me again?" Betty Lou said annoyed.

"Nope. I spared no expense." I handed her a box wrapped in gold foil.

"What is it?"

"Kind of ruins the point of wrapping the gift, don't you think?"

Betty Lou always loses her uptightness when she opens presents and she tore into the wrapping paper with the enthusiasm of a toddler.

Sis smiled when she opened the box and saw the teddy bear. "You got me Snazzy!"

"I did. It took a lot to find and get him back."

"Right, eBay is so hard to use."

"I didn't buy a copy. I had the original restored."

"You did not. As cute as this guy is, he's not the original Snazzy. How could he be?"

"I ended up having to rescue Santa and a yeti kid from an evil toymaker after finding the original."

"You're kidding right?"

"Nope."

"So is that the second time you saved Christmas?"

"Third actually. Helped deliver the presents too."

"What presents? Christmas isn't for months."

"Not here on Earth."

"I can't tell when you're kidding."

"I never kid about Christmas. But I am sorry it took me this long to replace Snazzy. I didn't realize it meant that much to you. I hope you can forgive me."

"Only if you hug and kiss Snazzy first," Betty Lou said with a sadistic grin. As a kid, she would make the entire family hug and kiss her teddy bear before she'd go to bed.

"Seriously?"

"I never kid about Snazzy."

"C'mon, Bikini. I won't bite you. Not again," said the bear.

"Did Snazzy just talk?" Betty Lou asked.

"Yep. Did I forget to mention that Snazzy is alive now? And has all the memories of the time you spent together as a kid?"

The stuffed bear turned his head toward me. "Alive is right. Next time you put someone in a box as a present, make sure you make the air holes bigger, Bikini."

"Sorry about that," I said.

"Now what about my kiss?"

Fine. I leaned over and gave the bear a peck on the top of his head.

"But how did you find him to restore? And how did he come to life? Is he safe?"

"Of course, I'm safe. Would inspector 23 lie and put on a fake label?" Snazzy said.

I saw the panic start in her eyes before it spread to the rest of her face. "Mary Sue…"

My assistant Stanley waved at me from near the podium.

"Sorry, Sis. Got to go."

I left Betty Lou and her bear to get reacquainted, walked behind the podium, and adjusted the microphone.

"I'd like to thank you all for coming and hope that

you're enjoying yourselves. Now it's time for a very special portion of our evening–the Bikini Foundation's Hero Award. The BFHA is given out only on rare occasions when someone does something truly above and beyond. Our latest recipient may look a trifle unusual but without this hero, there would be six fewer people…" And yes, I was technically stretching the definition here for Jenny but as far as I was concerned, she was still a person regardless of her form. "… alive in this room. This hero returned four young women to their bodies and gave a fifth a new lease on life in an alien form. Not only that, but he risked his own life to save that of his colleague from a clear and present danger. Ladies and gentlemen, I'd like you to put your hands together as we call up the recipient of the BFHA–Mr. Cuddles." The room thundered with applause. The four women, back in their bodies, were on their feet and screaming like they were at a rock concert. Jenny made the screeching clicking noise of the Quid. Doggy Dendrite simply stood there stunned.

"Me!?" he whispered.

"Mr. Cuddles, you're a hero!" cheered his daughter, Harper, but Dendrite just stood frozen on four legs, too shocked to move.

Dr. "Gibby" Gibson ran over and put Dendrite on his shoulders so he could carry him to the front of the room and place *Mr. Cuddles* on the stage. At the back of the podium, I'd had little stairs installed so doggy Dendrite could walk right up to the microphone.

"I don't know what to say, which is very unusual for me. I never expected anything like this. I am no hero. I wouldn't even have been a part of this had Bikini and Harper not cajoled me into it."

"That might be true, but you still became a hero," I said, holding up the award, a crystal star. The mechanical arms popped out from Mr. Cuddles's collar as he accepted the plaque.

"Thank you for this honor, Bikini. I will strive to be worthy of the BFHA." He looked down and saw he was listed as Mr. Cuddles. The former mad scientist smiled and winked at me. "I would like to dedicate it to the person who has inspired me to become a better person–Harper Dennis."

The applause confused him. Dendrite flipped the microphone switch off. "Thank you for giving the award to me as Mr. Cuddles, but you know better than anyone that I am not a *hero*."

"You weren't, but this once, you became one. However, being a hero once doesn't make you one forever. It is something that must be worked on every day. And when there are setbacks, a hero needs to keep striving to be better."

"Even you?"

"Especially me. Someday Harper is going to find out who you really are and the stuff you did in the past. But this, and what you choose to do from here on out, will show her the man, or dog, that you became for her."

"You have given me a lot to think about."

"Let me give you something else to think about–a job with Bikini Enterprises."

"I can't commit to that. I need to have my time free to look out for Harper."

"She's a kid. That's not a full-time job."

"Not yet it isn't." That didn't sound ominous at all. "But consider me a consultant for when things like this happen."

"I will." Before I could ask him more about the *not yet* statement, Harper came over and grabbed the dog with her father's brain.

"C'mon Mr. Cuddles. Let's dance."

She carried doggy Dendrite in her arms and they spun around the dance floor. Betty Lou was holding Snazzy the teddy bear the same way as they tangoed. Stanley and Hany were dancing up a storm.

Jenny and the other former Quid were cutting a rug with Sherman, our cyborg octogenarian doorman. Jenny was holding his hands with her tentacles and spinning Sherman around so fast that his legs had lifted off the ground.

I couldn't blame them. The music was provided by Rock 'n Roll Heaven. A music executive had cloned the bodies of some of the greatest deceased musicians in the world–including Elvis, Frank Sinatra, Jimi Hendrix, Mozart, Beethoven, Louie Armstrong, Howling Wolf, Biggie, Prince, and John Lennon. This wouldn't have been a bad thing if he hadn't made a deal with Legba to reincarnate the souls of the originals into the new bodies and then try to kill thousands of music fans. I joined them in a battle of the bands that was more of an actual battle. We won and saved the fans. Something in the afterlife had convinced them to not want to return to the limelight, so they played small venues just for the sake of the music. They are kind enough to play my parties.

Glass pleaded guilty and gotten life in prison with no chance of parole. I guess my sister could bluff as well as I could.

I stood off in the corner, happy just to watch everyone else have a good time.

"Ms. Jones, this just won't do," Sherman said, coming up alongside me.

"What won't do, Sherman?"

"You being off here in the corner by your lonesome."

"I'm not alone," I said, motioning to the crowd dancing to the music of legends. My smile broadened as I watched Jenny the Quid use her telekinesis to lift

Snazzy and Mr. Cuddles so the three of them floated and danced in the air. "It's times like these I realize just how lucky I am in my life. I like making sure I take the time to appreciate it."

"I understand," Sherman said, then stood and whistled for several moments. "Are you done?"

"I suppose."

"Good." Sherman bowed and extended his elbow to me. "Now would you do an old man the honor of a jitterbug?"

I put my hand in the crook of his arm. "I would love to."

There has long been a debate among certain obscure and drunken literary scholars about whether **PATRICK THOMAS** was raised by Cthulhu, a leprechaun in a Manhattan bar, or two human parents. What there is no arguing about is that Patrick is the award-winning author of 40 books including the beloved fantasy humor *Murphy's Lore series* (9 books from *Tales from Bulfinche's Pub* to *The Mug Life*), as well as 2 books in the future space adventures in the *Startenders* series.

The Murphy's Lore After Hours spin-offs star the half pixie/ogre Terrorbelle (*Fairy With A Gun, Fairy Rides The Lightning,* and *Terrorbelle The Unconquered*); the former demon-possessed serial killer Agent Karver of the Department of Mystic Affairs (*Dead To Rites, Rites of Passage*); the cursed magí Hex (*By Darkness Cursed* and *By Invocation Only*); Vince Argus, the Soul For Hire (*Greatest Hits*); and Negral, a forgotten Sumerian god who works as Hell's Detective (*Lore & Dysorder, Bullets & Brimstone,* and the graphic novel *The Moon Maniac* with Blair Webb).

His *Mystic Investigators* paranormal mystery series includes *Shadows & Brimstone* (omnibus of *Bullets & Brimstone* and *From The Shadows* with John French), *Once Upon In Crime* (omnibus of *Once More Upon A Time* and *Partners In Crime* with Diane Raetz) *Mystic Investigators,* and *Mean Streets. Assassins' Ball* is his first traditional mystery, co-written with John French. He co-edited *Camelot 13, New Blood, Hear Them Roar* and was an editor for the magazines *Fantastic Stories of the Imagination* and *Pirate Writings.*

His other works include the steampunk *As The Gears Turn.* the space epic *Exile & Entrance,* and the *Bikini Jones* series. Patrick's darkly humorous advice column *Dear Cthulhu* has been running since 2005 and has 6 collections including *Cthulhu Knows Best* and *What Would Cthulhu Do?* The Dear Cthulhu advice empire has expanded from magazines and books to radio as Dear Cthulhu now broadcasts monthly on the show Destinies: The Voice of Science Fiction which is hosted by Dr. Howard Margolin.

Over 100 of his stories have been published in magazines and anthologies. His noir novella appears in *Murder in Montague Falls.* A number of his books were part of the props department of the CSI television show and *Nightcaps* was even thrown at a suspect's head. His urban fantasy *Fairy With A Gun* had been optioned for film and TV by Laurence Fishburne's Cinema Gypsy Productions. Top Men Productions has turned his *Soul For Hire* Story, *Act of Contrition,* into a short film.

He also writes books for kids as PATRICK T. FIBBS including the *Undead Kid Diaries: Over My Dead Body, the Babe B. Bear Mysteries: Bad Hair Day, Joy Reaper Checks Out,* and *the Ughabooz* picture book *5 Silly Monsters Jumping On The Zed* and early reader *Soggy Goes to the Beach.*

Please drop by www.patthomas.net or follow him at I_PatrickThomas at Twitter or www.facebook.com/PatrickThomasAuthor to learn more.

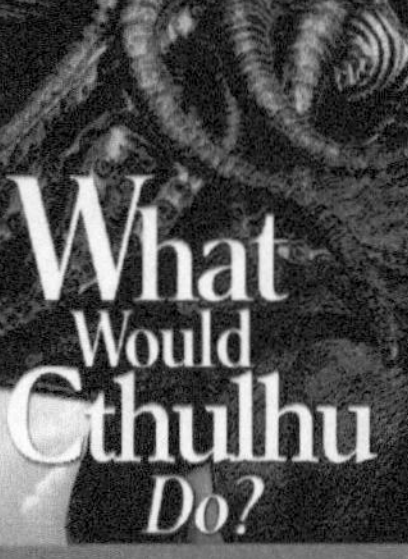

DEAR CTHULHU

The advice column to **END** all advice columns

WWW.DEARCTHULHU.COM
WWW.PADWOLF.COM

More GREAT Science Fiction!

THE STARSCAPE PROJECT

As his quest begins, an artificial intelligence life form enters the galaxy and launches a series of covert attacks against the Empire. The Teconeans assume that the Federation is responsible, and galactic peace is about to unravel. As Stryker chases his nemesis into Teconean space, he finds himself thrown into the middle of the battle. Knowing that Earth will be the aliens' next target, Stryker must decide whether to let them destroy the Empire, or to join forces with his Teconean enemies against the invaders. The key to the mysterious aliens lies buried on the moon of Kennedy Prime, and it's up to Stryker to solve the puzzle before war benins. The fate of the galaxy is at stake.

ZONE OF THE TENTH DGREE

1912, an alien ship crash lands in the Atlantic ean, setting up a secret colony that remains detected for centuries, allowing them to nipulate some of the most important events in man history -- from the sinking of the Titanic to Bermuda triangle to global warming. Now, technology of the 26th century has covered the aliens' distress beacon, and it's a e against time as the Navy tries to stop a rorist armed with a nuclear weapon from stroying the colony and triggering an all-out r as the mother-ship approaches

Now available from
PADWOLF PUBLISHING
visit padwolf.com

A detective's work is never done
And don't call him Baby Bear...

NO TEACHERS. NO PARENTS SCHOOL IS OUT.... OF THIS WORLD

15th Aniversary
Omnibus of
Books 1-6

The zombie apocalypse is over...

Now even undead kids have to go to school

5 SILLY MONSTERS JUMPING ON THE ZED

a picture book
for kids

www.talehaven.com

DOWN THESE
MEANS STREETS
of Magic & Monsters walk the

MYSTIC INVESTIGATORS

www.ingramcontent.com/pod-product-compliance
Lightning Source LLC
Chambersburg PA
CBHW031418200726
48285CB00017BA/2471